The Mystery Box

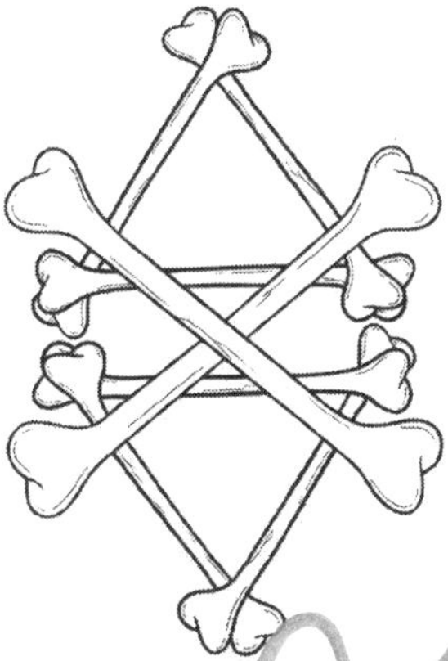

Kay Schutte

For permission requests, please contact Kay Schutte at:
kayschutte11@hotmail.com

For bulk ordering, please contact Kay Schutte at:
kayschutte11@hotmail.com

Written by Kay Schutte
Edited by Jorie Tash
Interior Formatting by Nicolas Beron
Cover Art by Jess Smith @jayy.smith.design

First edition 2024
Paperback ISBN: 979-8-218-42586-9

Dedication

To Brenda, Turtle, Bette and Mick

Thank you for always believing in and supporting me,
no matter what crazy dream spews out of my head.

TABLE OF CONTENTS

CHAPTER 1

"Hey everyone! Especially my they/them peeps! This, as always, is my beautiful partner and sidekick-in-crime, Hayden. Today is going to be a very special spooky episode of Put Up or Shut Up because we just hit 500,000 subscribers!" I say to the glowing red camera light as Jameson stares at his phone when he's obviously supposed to be directing us.

Hayden jumps in and says, "With all of the likes, shares and subscriber's we were able to collect enough money to do a video we've been dying ***WINK WINK*** to do for the longest time." Hayden is literally my dream girl, with her dirty blonde hair and ocean gray eyes that glow from her lightly freckle-frosted face. She makes me want to melt with her light blue holey skinny jeans, her black cropped tank, and that single pair of black, doodled-on Chucks she's worn since her college dorm days--without wanting to show off too much of her emo phase, some traces can't help but remain. Hayden found me one fall day when it felt to me like the sun would never rise and put that goofy crooked smile back on my boyish face.

I feel a light elbow to my ribs and realize it's my turn to talk and stop staring at the love of my life instead.

"Pause," I say. "Jameson, you need to be helping us, man. This is our biggest episode to date."

"Relax," Jameson says, "We haven't even gotten the box yet."

"Well, it's ordered, and we should have it in just a few days," I answered. "I know we aren't allowed tracking from that sketchy-as-fuck website, but we need to be prepared. The intro to this video is important, because when we do get the box, it's going to be a long night."

I've always been hyper-fixated on organization—I imagine that goes back 10 years to when I was 19 in a metal band, trying to make it big. I always had to be the manager. I would do everything and anything to get us to the big leagues. Sometimes I mistake being a psychotic control-freak with passion. Hayden always tells me, "Parker, it's okay to let things be. You can't always control every aspect of my feelings or other people's feelings." I admit she's right, but at the same time, I can't always swallow my damn pride. Maybe my penchant for running the show is related to my parents splitting up after they had me as high schoolers, cutting my hair, questioning my gender, or dropping out of college. Hayden loves me for me, regardless--for my Spider-Man tattooed arms, the holes in my ears, the giant scar across my chest, and that goofy smile I mentioned.

"Makes sense. I'm sorry, shithead." Jameson says in a teasing voice. We've been friends since we toured the country together five years ago. He's like the blood brother that I never had. I promise to never get tired of calling him a fuckface if he never gets tired of calling me a shithead. Jameson has been our man behind the camera since Hayden and I decided to start doing queer videos during the Covid lockdown. We were so overcome with boredom after we were both laid off from our dead-end jobs that we started making short videos, and we got a lot of traction from our queer family all over the world. It has made a nice little blanket of income to help pay for our small apartment, our pup, vacations and food. We don't need much else. We really only need each other. Jameson, on the other hand, is ALL about the new flashy camera gear and shoes, though that pales in comparison to his obsession with watches (and I've never seen him use any of those he wears on his tiny wrist to actually tell the time). We pay him a good fair chunk of our Put Up or Shut Up earnings, and he also has his own fan page. (Don't let that get to his head. He doesn't need another God complex.) He's also always accepted Hayden with open arms, maybe because he was the one who had to drag me out of the hell where I spent the summer before I met her, and I think he can see how happy she makes me. That summer I could barely eat or sleep. I walked around like a damn zombie, thought about ending it right then and there. But alas, remember, she paints that goofy-ass smile on my face constantly.

"Press record, fuckface." I say. Once the red camera light pops back on again, I say, "You all know Halloween is mine and Hayden's favorite holiday, so we reached out to a person who wishes to remain anonymous, and they helped us access the dark web."

Hayden jumps in. "So, this place was totally insane. You can buy guns, drugs, nightmare-inducing porn, literally anything. Even illegal fruits, which gave me a good chuckle! Did you know some types of plums used in wine are sold on the black market because they're illegal in the United States? Wild!"

I grin. "It's so crazy, but what we were really after was a dark-web mystery box. I know, I know: we aren't the first people to go on the dark web and get a mystery box. But! We saved up $500,000 and sought out this anonymous person to get the best and darkest mystery box our money could buy."

"So, stay tuned! This video is sponsored by Whitcom Industries, who helped us with a massive donation to do this video." Hayden says.

"Let's open the box!" I say. Jameson shuts off the camera, the red light extinguished.

"So, what's with this Whitcom sponsorship?" Jameson asks.

"I'm really not sure," I admit. "I just got a random email one day saying they wanna sponsor a video and sent a money wire of about $500,000. I mean, we've had plenty of sponsorships before, but with that much money just landing in a bank account I just opened, well, I wasn't going to question it, and they didn't want anything more than a shoutout in the video."

Hayden's worried eyes are boring straight through me.

"I don't know about this, Parker. It's really weird that they just sent you all this money wanting nothing in return."

"Babe, I know it's weird, but we need this. This is the video that can really set us up for the rest of our lives." Glancing at Jameson, "All three of our lives," I added.

I know Hayden and Jameson think I have zero patience, and, well, maybe I don't. When I get an idea in my mind, I want to go through with it. I need to see how it plays out. Even if it flops (and I've had plenty of flops, especially in the music industry). I guess the kids nowadays would say I have the "'tism." So yes, I do hyper fixate on projects. I admit it. But this one--I just have a gut feeling this is going to work out. It needs to work out.

"Alright, my friends, I'm outta here! I got a nice little date with this girl I met on a dating app. She's pretty fucking cool and we're going out for ramen," Jameson says as he starts packing up the camera gear and cables. "Please let me know when the box comes in. Even if it comes Thursday, I'll be here Friday for the opening. But dude, enough about the box. Check out our cute-as-hell texts we've been sending each other!"

Jameson shows me his phone and the plethora of messages he and his so-called girl have been sending back and forth for a couple days now. They've obviously been flirting.

Jameson: I cannot wait for our date tomorrow!

Scarlett: Me either :)

Jameson: You're not a murder or something right? Just a cute girl wanting to meet this hunk?

I start rolling my eyes.

Scarlett: There's no promises handsome ;)

I throw the phone back in Jameson's hands and say, "Ew, you two are already gross. But for sure, asshat, I'll let you know when we get the box. Love you, man, and I hope you have a great date. I can't wait to have double dates in the future!"

"Bye, Jameson! See you soon! I also hope your date goes well!" Hayden calls out. Jameson walks out the front door of my apartment, his silver, probably-overpriced watch catching the hallway light as he exits.

Hayden moved in after a year of us dating. Jameson and I split the spot before, but he knew it was time to move on. He bought a nice little condo on the West Side of Denver right by my favorite brewery. To say I'm a little jealous is an understatement, but my place with Hayden isn't too shabby. We split a two-bedroom apartment where we sleep on a queen-sized bed with our French bulldog, Boba, in the room we deemed the master. We turned Jameson's former bedroom into our own personal studio after he moved out. That's where we record most of our videos. It's basically our office, but for the most fun job in the entire world: being silly with my girl. I still can't believe I don't need a day job anymore. I had been struggling delivering pizza before the pandemic hit while Hayden was trying to climb the corporate latter with the business degree she obtained from

Montana State. She always had her life together, so much more than I. I fell into the music and hated school, where she went right from high school in 2011 before eventually graduating. She jumped into her first job as an assistant junior manager of a corporation that was in control of a new type of tech that flopped. After that, it was hard to find a job during lockdown.

As I start putting cords away, Hayden suddenly pulls me into an embrace and says, "This is so spooky, but I'm really happy we get the chance to do this together. As far as we know, everything in the box is just going to be fake like the other ones."

I laugh and say, "Baby, it will probably be a bunch of clothes soaked in fake blood and maybe some dead bugs that smell bad, but our job is to make it seem really real, right? We're good at that, and it's for the views and our livelihood! I think Whitcom just wants some Google searches, found our videos and think that we're going to reach their audience. If they are a Halloween horror store, I think they made the right move!"

I can feel Hayden laugh through our embrace.

She smiles, flashing her perfectly straight teeth, kisses me, and says "Alright, let's clean up and make some dinner. We have to remember to take Boba to the vet tomorrow for his nail trim." Boba looks up at us at the sound of his name and then rolls on his back like a worm for belly rubs.

The next morning, I wake up like any other ordinary day. Hayden is still asleep, as I usually wake up about an hour before she does. She sprawls on stage left of the bed, snoring lightly, but Boba is ready to get up with me. We leave her be and strut to the coffee maker. While my toffee nut coffee is brewing, I decide to check my phone, like any millennial would do right when they wake up, and I see I have an urgent email from my leasing office. It states:

PARKER JOHNSON

WE NEED YOUR IMMEDIATE ATTENTION TO THE LEASING OFFICE AS A PACKAGE HAS ARRIVED WITH A VERY UNIQUE SMELL. PLEASE HEAD DOWN AT YOUR EARLIEST CONVIENIENCE.

THANKS CIRCA FITZ COMPLEX

I instantly forget about my coffee, throw on Boba's monster harness (that is so cute you just want to pinch his cheeks like a little baby), and head down the stairs across the parking lot to the leasing office. A skinny man with brown hair who I've never seen before greets me and says, "How can I help you?"

"I'm Parker Johnson, and I just got an email about a package."

The man stares at me for a little too long before his cheeks seem to reach up to his ears in a very strange--almost pained--smile and says, "Oh yes, I decided to email you before management got here, they would've been very displeased with the smell of your package."

"Yeah, I'm sorry about that." I say. "I can take it off your hands now."

The man's eyes go very dark, the strange rictus grin still painted on his face, and he stares at me for what feels like an eternity. "One second," as the man steps back, grabs the package and hands it to me.

"Have a great day," he says to me.

"Thanks," I murmur. "Let's go, Boba."

As I'm halfway out the door, I swear I hear him say, "8721."

I turn around only to see that there was no one standing at the front desk anymore.

I say to Boba, “Well, that was fucking weird,” as Boba just stares up at me with his tongue curled, ready to walk back to the apartment.

As I get back upstairs, I instantly throw the box in the corner of the living room, the corner where we would put our Christmas tree. I sit back on the couch, not even thinking about the coffee I just made, but it’s probably cold now, anyway. The door to our room creaks open, and I see out of my peripheral vision Hayden, her hair up in a bun, with one of my giant brewery logo shirts on, and maybe underwear too, but the shirt is too big to tell. I don’t stop staring at the box.

She yawns and says, “Why the fuck does the coffee smell like that, Parker? It’s not like you can burn it using a Keurig.”

She stops in her tracks, her eyes following my line of sight to the box in the corner, and breathes, “That’s it, isn’t it?”

“Yeah.” I say. “Sorry. There’s cold coffee on the counter. The leasing office said I had to come get it because of the smell.” I couldn’t take my eyes off the box. It seemed like it stared right back at me with a million invisible eyes.

Hayden starts opening windows. Luckily, October in Colorado isn’t a million degrees.

“It’s only Wednesday. I’m not sure we can let that box just rot in the corner until Friday. The neighbors are going to call a wellness check on us thinking our corpses are just rotting away in here and Boba is feasting on our remains.” Hayden says, breaking my trance.

“Stop,” I say through a small smile. “Boba would never eat his favorite parent, AKA me, would you, Boba?” He looks at me, but doesn’t answer. Encouraging.

Hayden rolls her eyes and says, "Seriously, Parker, we need to either get this done or just throw the box away."

"Are you fucking serious?" I say, annoyed. "Whitcom funded this HALF-A-MILLION-DOLLAR box and literally went onto the dark web to get it for us. We have to do this video."

"Is there something you're not telling me?" Hayden says. "You don't have to yell at me, Parker."

"No, baby. I'm really sorry." I feel bad. "This just means a lot to me. I really think we're going to break the freaking internet with the combination of this box and our sparkling personalities. I really just... want this to work. It's Halloween, our favorite holiday. Let's just be spooky together. I'm really sorry I raised my voice."

Hayden sighs and says, "Just call Jameson and get him over here."

CHAPTER 2

"Jameson, you need to come over right now," I say into my phone. "It doesn't matter. You need to get over here right now and help us record this video. The box smells so bad, dude. Okay, okay, okay, she can come."

"What?" Hayden says as I just look at her and roll my eyes. I put the speaker of the phone to my chest and say, "He won't come over unless that girl that he went on a date with comes. He says they had the best time last night and she's the one," as I pretend to gag about it. I put the phone back to my ear.

"Yeah, yeah, I'm here. Jameson, just bring her over and just make sure she's quiet." Hayden clicks her tongue and says, "Jameson is an idiot, bringing some random girl over to film a YouTube video. I bet she's great and all, but this is like his job. 'Bring your girlfriend to work day' it is!"

About an hour later, Jameson calls me to buzz him up. Hayden and I have already been eating too much Advil because the stench of the box is giving us both a headache. Jameson doesn't knock, just walks right in, immediately slips his mouth and nose under the collar of his shirt, and shouts, "Dude, that box is god-awful. It smells just like when I used to work at this place called the Ally Rally and this dude brought a huge dresser full of shit to dump, but I swear to God, there was a dead body in it. There's probably a fucking dead body in that box, bro!"

"Shut up," I say to Jameson, "This is all probably for show. Who knows what we're going to find when we actually start filming? Speaking of filming, get the camera set up, man."

Jameson nods and says, "Oh, and guys, by the way, this is Scarlett. You ruined our second date." Scarlett also has her nose and mouth covered with the collar of her blue crew neck. She has beautiful brown curly hair. She's wearing plain Vans, jeans, and visible cutting scars.

"No, no, no, that's totally okay!" Scarlett says brightly. "This sound way more fun and interesting, anyways! I promise, I will be no bother. Just Jameson's helper."

Hayden crosses the living room and politely says, "It's totally okay, the more the merrier! It might get a little crazy in here so we need all the hands we can get."

We bring the box into our little studio, which is blacked out with heavy curtains. The box is about the size of a moving box, one that you would put your kitchen pots and pans into. The corners are stained with a damp sheen, kind of like oil has been spilled on the edges. It's also duct-taped in every which way. We set the box on the table and put two chairs behind it for myself and my amazing co-host.

"Alright, Jameson. Let's go," I say as he counts down on his five fingers until there were none remaining. I again meet the camera's red Cyclopean eye, and I realize, finally, this is it!

Remembering we had already filmed the introduction of the video, I say "The dark web mystery box is here! Just gotta tell you guys: it smells awful. My camera man Jameson told me it smells exactly like a dead body, so let's see about that."

Hayden jumps in and says, "Please, you guys, don't try this at home. We're already scared ourselves and we took precautions. First, we have gloves, masks, and water for anything that could get on our skin or in our lungs. Second, we did make sure that our cell phones are working and the internet connection is solid in case we have to get the authorities involved."

"But that wouldn't be any fun. So, let's get started!" I shout. I can see Hayden already getting very tense and a little annoyed with me, but I'm not very patient, remember? I give her leg a small apologetic squeeze below the camera's line of sight. She nudges me back a little, and I think we're good and ready to go.

"Let's get these gloves on," I proclaim, as I feel the tight stretch of the latex struggling to get over my already-sweaty hands. I snap the bottom of my glove like I'm a doctor on Grey's Anatomy and start opening the box with a kitchen knife. Hayden is taking small shallow breaths, either due to her apprehension or to avoid breathing in the stench blooming out of the box.

"I think I can do this without the mask, but guys, like I said, the stench is unreal." I say.

As I finally get the box flaps to pop open, I slyly say, "Ladies first?" to Hayden. She just rolls her eyes and nods.

"Alrighty, first grab and we have... what looks like a tiny ring box. Okay. Let's get to opening it, I guess." Hayden chuckles slightly. "Oh my God, this is already disgusting."

"What is it, let me see and show our audience!" I say excitedly.

"It's just a wooden ring box of full of clipped fingernails. But there's also something carved in the top of the box."

Hayden shows the camera the strange carving at the top of the box. It's two triangles, but the bottoms are almost touching each other. One right side up, the other upside down. There's an "x" cutting through the whole thing on top of the triangles.

"I've never seen that kind of symbol before, but it honestly may mean nothing. Could just be to scare us," I say. "My turn!"

My hands are shaking from excitement as I pull the next item out of the box.

"It looks like just a small Micky Mouse blanket," I say. I continue to inspect the blanket, turning it over in my hands and holding it up to the light, and find an almost-damp spot, dark red, right on the top of Micky's left ear.

"That's definitely blood." Hayden squeaks out.

"Yeah, you're right. And it's also still kind of wet, too." I say, making a sick face. My instincts tell me to just reach in again, so I do. I pull out a piece of paper that looks like a blank receipt.

"Alright, guys, this is a little less scary, but only because it's not bloody. I just pulled out this weird-looking paper, and it has writing on it." I say. I hold the note up to the camera.

COME FIND ME

39.748383

-104.873029

"That has to be longitude and latitude, right?" Hayden says.

"Yeah. I mean, I think. I would assume so, but I was never one for getting any good grades in geography class," I try and laugh the creepy note off with a joke.

"Parker, I just Googled it, and that's literally a house in downtown Denver." Hayden says.

"No fucking way, this has to be some random house they just found on Google Maps and they're just trying to scare us," shouts Jameson from behind the camera.

"Dude, you're not supposed to be talking. We're filming right now, man," I say, overprotective of my show.

"Yeah, I'll cut this part out, Parker, but I mean, don't you think that's kind of weird? This mystery box is supposed to be random; it could've come from anywhere in the entire world, and it came from someone 20 minutes from your apartment?"

"We won't know unless we go find out!" I say.

"Parker, shut up. We aren't going to go 'find out'," Hayden says, punctuating her impression of me with air quotes.

"Okay, fine. Can we just keep looking in the box and finish this video before I have a permanent headache from either Jameson or the smell?" I concede.

Hayden laughs and nods.

"Your turn, babe," I say, pushing the box ever-so-lightly toward her.

Hayden reaches in and pulls out a plastic baggie holding a syringe filled with a grey-looking liquid.

"I'm so glad I didn't just stab myself with this needle," Hayden says as she throws the bag onto the table.

The grey liquid looks as if it came right out of a Marvel comic. It swirls in the tube just like the contents of an old lava lamp you would find on the shelves of a Walmart in 2003. My brain starts going into a fog, into something like a daydream, and I start to think about my childhood in my grandma's old house. My mom's room was downstairs, and I vividly remember wanting the lava lamp to just turn on already. I remember wanting so desperately to touch it, even though the glass was actually as hot as lava. Being so little, it felt like an eternity for that lava to warm enough to actually start floating, and I would just stare, mesmerized. Maybe that's where my lack of patience started. Maybe this tactic is a way for my brain to try and not to be scared to finish going through the box. At that, my mind drifts back to the box and where we are, and I can hear Hayden asking, "Parker, do you have any thoughts about this weird liquid?"

I snap back to reality and say, "I literally have no idea, but it looks really freaking cool, don't you think? Comment and tell us your thoughts on what this mystery liquid is! Also, before we go any further, I do want to give another shoutout to Whitcom Industries for helping us with this video, from the funding all the way to helping us get the mystery box from the dark web. We couldn't have done this without you!"

I plunge my hand back in the mystery box, thinking that all of us have probably gone very noseblind to the smell by now. You can only smell things for so long before it's just a part of the furniture, right? I pull out a round object covered in kitchen washcloths, but, out of the corner of my eye, I suddenly notice Scarlett. I think about her promise to stay quiet and realize she's doing a very good job at keeping it, but she's also got this sly smile on her face. I think maybe she's just having a good time with new friends. I mean, this is probably the best way to meet people, watching them do stupid things.

I met most of my friends by doing said stupid things. We would go ding-dong ditching and get the cops called on us almost every weekend. We would go through drive-throughs and order one ice cream cone. Then we would grab the cone from the ice cream part and not the cone. The workers were probably so over our teenage shit. They definitely don't get paid enough to deal with that. Don't even get me started with the marshmallow gun we would run around with and shoot drunk people on the street.

"Alright, guys, this thing is wrapped in, like, a million kitchen washcloths," I say as I start unwrapping them one by one for added suspense. As I get to the last washcloth, I begin to see the blood soaking through. Before I know it, I am holding in my hand a bloody organ, almost like a liver or a kidney, but brutally mangled. What lays beside it is a human ear which, judging by the ragged edges, looks to have been removed from its owner with a small saw. So, this is where the smell was coming from: decomposing human body parts. Everyone in the room gasps as Hayden tries to swallow her vomit.

No one says a word for what feels like an eternity before I swallow hard and say, "Okay, guys, this appears to be an organ, while this is... literally a human ear. It's probably nothing, guys. Let's just keep going."

"Are you fucking serious, Parker?" Jameson says, incredulous. "That's too much. We should be done. We should call the cops."

I glare at him and say "Okay, guys. I didn't want to tell you this, but we can't call the cops. It's literally in the contract I signed with Whitcom Industries. We would be sued for over a million dollars if we involve the authorities." I know this doesn't sound great. "This is great, actually," I say. "We're going to get so many views with this weird shit!"

"Don't you realize after we post this on the internet maybe the cops will find out and someone will be knocking on our door sooner or later?" Hayden yells.

"I do realize that, and that's not breaking the contract! It states that if one of us contacts the police then we're fucking broke for the rest of our lives, but I read it in depth enough to confirm it says nothing about what would happen if the authorities find the video and come asking questions, okay?" I reply. "Just keep filming, but we won't talk to the audience. We'll just see what else is in the box together and be done, alright?"

For the first time since we began filming, Scarlett speaks, and she says, "Come on, Jameson,' where's the fun in just quitting? I won't be able to sleep unless we figure out what the rest of the box holds."

"See, even your girl's on my side!" I joke.

"Shut up and go." Jameson says while gently drawing his fingers across Scarlett's arm.

"There're only a couple things left in the box, anyway," I say, as I pull out two thumb drives. "Alright, cool, these aren't that scary."

"What's scary is probably whatever's on them," says Hayden. "In most videos they look at thumb drives and disks either last or in a whole separate video, it's kind of like a part two and I hate that."

"Let's just look at them now," I say.

"I'll go get the laptop." Jameson says.

I start to wonder how we're going to get the perfect shot of the video for the audience, but I also promised we could now all be in this together. My brain starts turning: maybe this could turn into more of a documentary rather than just a YouTube video.

Jameson brings the laptop over and goes back behind the camera.

"Okay, let's just all sit behind the computer in the shot," I say. I'll screen record it so we can put it like a reaction video on the top left while still seeing all of our faces. Even you, Scarlett. Just come sit by us. We will get a couple more chairs."

"You sure about this, Parker?" Hayden whispers while I start getting up. "You usually want this to be perfect, you want to be the star in control."

I laugh a little bit because I know she means no harm and say, "Gotta let go some time, right?"

Once we get everyone situated, Jameson stands up and presses record on the camera. In my mind, I imagine the red light illuminating everyone's faces perfectly, like a scene in a Valentine's Day movie. We pop the first thumb drive in.

"What if this absolutely wrecks your laptop, Jameson?" Hayden asks.

"Well, I bought this laptop with our first payment from the Put Up or Shut Up channel because I knew we would need it for editing, and that's all I do on it. Thankfully, there's no personal information on there, so, I mean, if it were just a huge malware attack or hacker then all they would get are files upon files of videos of us. Which, as you know, you can just find on our channel!" Jameson says proudly.

"Smart Jameson!" I say, as I gave him a pat on the back. "I'm glad you believed in our channel from the start. You're a good friend."

"Stop trying to sweeten me up, Parker, I'm here for the rest of the box. You don't have to get all lovey-dovey on me now."

I roll my eyes as the computer recognizes there's been a thumb drive inserted. I double-click to open it, and everyone seemingly holds our breath together while it loads. What we then see is a photo album of about 15 pictures. It starts with a skyline view of downtown Denver and slowly zooms in. These pictures must be about 20ish years old, what with the grainy quality you can see on the film. I also realize the pictures are that old because half of those skyscrapers in the downtown area are no longer visible. This would have to be a brilliant Photoshop, otherwise. The pictures keep zooming and zooming until we hit a spot by the train tracks.

"I know that place," Scarlett says. "Those are the train tracks a couple blocks from where I work. It's almost impossible to walk over there without jumping the tracks because of the light rail and all the actual trains escorting whatever BSN escorts."

Everyone was slightly confused as to where these pictures were taking us. We clicked past the picture of the tracks until we scrolled to picture number 10. We see a small blue house on the side of the train tracks like it was just plopped there, with no other neighboring houses around.

"That's weird," Hayden says. "There's no way that house can still be there, with all the high-rise apartments in that area."

The next picture brings us to the front of the house. The blue paint is lightly peeling away from the house, which is placed behind a small grass area with a tiny metal fence. It looks just like a normal old house, with a light brown front porch and a white mailbox, but the photo is too grainy to make out the numbers. It has two small windows on each side and one placed on top where you could assume was an attic. The next two pictures are almost exactly the same, but there are some slight differences between them. The last picture didn't differ much from those preceding it, except that there was a man standing on the porch. He's seemingly in his 40s, and he's with a small little girl, maybe about eight years old, sitting on the steps. Beside her was also a boy with brown hair, seemingly in his early teens. The smog from the outgoing trains in the distance blur the scene. The photo isn't clear enough to see the color of their eyes, but the 40ish-year-old man held a cane in his hands. We clicked one more time, only to end back up at the start of the photos.

"Okay, then. A cute little family in Denver, sitting on the porch of a house that's probably destroyed now," Hayden says. "Weird, but not as scary as the literal fucking body parts sitting on the kitchen counter. Let's pop in the next drive!"

Everyone agrees while Jameson ejects the thumb drive and inserts the other.

We all wait patiently while the computer ponders the foreign object in its side. The thumb drive pops up on the screen, but we come to realize its password protected with a four-digit pin.

"Well, so much for that," Hayden says.

"Type in 1111," Jameson says.

"Not everyone is that dumb," Hayden proclaims while typing it into the empty field anyway. PASSWORD INCORRECT pops up on the screen. They all start trying random numbers; even Scarlett chimes in with some. The computer puts out PASSWORD INCORRECT over and over again while I just sit in silence.

At first, I'm secretly devastated that we can't access this thumb drive. I keep telling myself over and over in my head that we have enough footage and this isn't the end-all if we can't get this folder to open. I just have a gut feeling that this is going to throw us over the edge. I start thinking about the last drive and all the photos, especially the one with the people in it. The teenager gave me the weirdest gut feeling, like a stone was being shoved down my throat into my stomach. Even looking at that picture, my eyes started to water out of sheer fear. Just like my eyes water every time someone tells stories or shares pictures of a skinwalker or an abandoned building with a ghost.

Then it just hits me.

I had been so excited that the box had been delivered that I forgot that I opened up a P.O. box to get it sent to, so why the fuck did it come to my apartment? Why the fuck did I get an email from my complex saying that it was in the leasing office? Why the fuck was a guy I've never seen before handing it to me with that creepy pained smile?

I quietly say, "Try 8721."

No one is listening to me, so I yell, "Guys, please try 8721!" I grab the computer myself, type in those four secret numbers and it simply said...

ACCESS GRANTED.

CHAPTER 3

"Okay, okay, okay, I'm not going to freak out, but PARKER EXPLAIN RIGHT NOW." Hayden screams at me.

"Long story short, I had the box sent to a PO box that I opened up but totally forgot about, and it was sent here, instead. Some weird guy I've never seen before at our leasing office emailed me and gave it to me. It was the weirdest interaction, but I just assumed he was new and nervous and it was his first day or some shit like that. Then when I was leaving, he, like, whispered those four numbers, but when I turned around to ask 'what,' he was gone. Boba and I thought nothing of it. Actually, I hope Boba is okay sleeping in our room right now with the smell," I say.

"He's probably fine," Hayden says. "I can't believe you didn't tell me any of this." I frown and notice Jameson with his face in his hands and Scarlett just sitting there, trying not to join in on a fight of a couple she just met.

"Baby I'm really sorry. Can we just look at this folder?" I say trying to lighten the mood that is currently painted a starless midnight. Hayden shakes her head and clicks the folder open.

This thumb drive also consists of only a photo album, just like the last one. The first picture that pops open is of a stairwell going down into a basement. It honestly just looks like a creepy stairwell that you would see on any B-horror movie. I click to the next picture. It takes us down the stairwell into a very bright, white room that looks like an operating room. There's a stretcher bed with hand and foot cuffs on the side and, next to the bed, is a metal table full of tools and a single syringe. These photos also look old and grainy, and I can't tell the shape of the tools or the contents of the syringe. My gut feeling tells me it's the same syringe as the one we found in our box. Everyone stays silent as we keep scrolling through the pictures. This next picture takes us to what seems like a hallway outside of the white medical room. These pictures are lining up like we're viewing an apartment online, like when you press each circle on the floor and get a 3D tour of your soon-to-be-new-home without actually getting your ass up off the couch and going to view it in person.

I'm starting to get impatient (what else is new?) and press next on the hallway picture right away. Before Hayden can even finish groaning, "Parker, I was looking at that," the next picture is on the screen.

It looks like the photo was taken from the hallway door, and it shows a room with a tattered old twin mattress on the floor. Dishes of rotting food are haphazardly stacked on every available surface, and scurrying, feasting roaches can be seen even through the grain of the old photo. The filthy room is painted red, and a girl that looks between the ages of 16 and 20 slumps lifeless on a wooden chair with blood pouring from her head. It's hard to see where else the blood is coming from, as it blends in with the red paint of the wall. We can only assume that this girl is dead, and she was murdered in the same house that's about 20 minutes away from my house. Everyone is in shock, now fully believing how real this is.

There's a small part of me that wants to say, "Ha! I got you guys! I actually made this box and got all this stuff from Spirit Halloween, everything's fake! Even the check-out girl helped me stage this picture for you guys!" Maybe I just wish that was the real situation we were in, but no. We're in *this* now.

Jameson says, quietly, "Should we keep looking, guys? I mean, this is all pretty messed up." Hayden says, to my surprise, "I think we're obligated to keep going, don't you guys think? What if this guy is still murdering people? There are clues everywhere. We have to keep looking, we have to keep going."

My anxiety is itching to lighten to mood and yell, "That's my girl! The Scooby Doo gang is here to solve this mystery!", but instead I just nod and press the right arrow button to the next picture, a close-up of the left side of the dead girl's face. There is definitely blood everywhere, and its source is the gaping hole in the side of her head where her ear should've been. There is a 99 percent chance that that very ear is now on my kitchen counter.

"Fuck, do you guys think we are now accomplices to murder?" Jameson yells. Before anyone can stop me, I scroll through the pictures waiting to be seen. I need to see them before there's another debate. The next picture is of a different room, where there's a man hanging from a noose. I can see he is still alive, but barely. His toes are touching a chair so he has a tiny sliver of slack through which he could breathe. The right side of his abdomen had been cut open and stapled shut. I don't know if anyone else realized this, but I think one of his organs may also be sitting on my kitchen counter. The next four pictures were just four glowing numbers: 1657. I try and memorize them as best as I can before eventually just writing them down on my wrist with a Sharpie.

"Okay guys, I really don't know what to do. We can't go to the cops. They probably wouldn't even believe us or do anything," I say. "Let's just finish going through this mystery box and these pictures. I know this sounds really money hungry, but listen guys, if we go to the cops and they don't find anything or the house is abandoned or, worst case, not even there anymore, we're losing about a million dollars...each."

"EACH?" Jameson and Hayden say simultaneously.

"I feel like I've apologized a million times today, but yes, we're, for lack of a better term, fucked," I say. "But guys, don't you realize if we do this as a documentary now, we're going to make millions, can maybe even be heroes? We will be set for life. Please, just stay with me for a little longer, and I promise if things get too bad, we can call the cops."

"Things are pretty fucking bad already, dude," Jameson says.

I ignore him and take Hayden's hand, look her in the eyes and say, "Baby, this could be it. No more chasing the economy, no more wondering what happens if we lose our viewership, no more 'I might have to start doing Doordash.' We could finally get our dream house and go on our dream vacations. We can get all the puppies and kitties we could ever want. I just have this feeling that this is big. I know it's fucking scary, but, like you say, these people might need us. Denver might need us. Shit, the whole world might need us. We know how cops work; don't you remember the protests? We've already gone ACAB we can't go back on that, either. Also, guys," I start to look at all of them, "We've got each other, and that's really all we need."

They all sit in silence for what feels like forever. This feels like telling someone you're in love with them and they pause for that split second before saying it back.

Well, I for sure didn't get the 'I love you' back, because Jameson stood up and says, "Nope. Not this time, Parker. You're not getting me with the hero God-complex shit that gets us off.

I'm going to the bathroom, and then I'm going to get my phone and we're going to call the cops. I'm done."

Jameson gets up and heads out of the room as Scarlett follows him.

Hayden and I sit in awkward silence as she puts her hand on my knee and says, "Baby, I know you've wanted this so badly for so long, and believe me, I want it too. It's just that this is all really messed up and we have to go to the authorities. We have to try, even if they don't do anything. It's the right thing to do."

She gives me a kiss on the cheek and starts rubbing the back of my head. I know she knows how disappointed I am. She can feel those feelings like the best empath in human skin. I stare at the box while listening to Jameson and Scarlett talk in the living room. I haven't heard him pick up his phone yet, so I say to Hayden, "I'm just going to look at the last three things, okay? And then you guys win. I'll be done."

Hayden nods as if to say that's the least she can do for me at the moment. I take it for what it is and throw my hand back into the box.

What I pull out, in one big scoop, are three Beanie Babies from the early 2000s. These aren't like ordinary Beanie Babies, though, as they have zero beans in them and their characteristic heart-shaped tags had been ripped off. *Wow, I can't believe they tore the tag off of these Beanie Babies. Now they are absolutely worth shit and I don't even get to know their names,* I think absently to myself. Snapping my brain back to the present and its gruesome gifts, I start to examine the beanie babies more closely. One of them is a small cougar with grayish brown fur and blue eyes, my favorite animal. The cougar also has different-colored fur above his eyes to look like eyebrows. Boba has the same fur pattern. The second Beanie Baby was a normal tiger with green eyes, and the third was a black monkey with a curly tail. Even though they came in the box, these Beanie Babies look brand new, aside from the missing beans and tags. They smell, but only because of their proximity to the rotting body parts in the box. Otherwise, they were clean of stains or any dirt.

Hayden emits a sigh of relief, visibly thinking that this could be the best-case scenario for the final contents of this demon box. While I examined each Beanie Baby, it seemed like I could feel... *something* inside them in lieu of beans. I flipped them all over on their backs and saw each of their bellies had been cut and hand-sewn back together.

"We have to open them back up. Can you hand me the scissors, babe?"

Hayden hands me the scissors, and I begin lightly cutting open each string on the cougar's soft belly, one by one, like the plastic surgeon when he had his fingers dancing all around my chest. What I pulled out of the first Beanie Baby was one thick piece of rolled-up paper. I unfurled it to see a picture of a lady grocery shopping. She obviously had no idea her picture was getting taken.

It took me a minute for my thoughts to compile before Hayden yelled, "Oh my God, Parker, that's your fucking grandma."

To be honest, this was the first thing to make my heart completely stop and drop to the pit of my suddenly acid-filled stomach. Here in front of me was a picture of my grandma, unaware anything is wrong, just shopping at what is probably fucking Walmart in my shithole of a hometown. Hayden rips open the second Beanie Baby, the tiger, to find a picture of her mother and father having their nightly walk down their HOA-secured neighborhood to pick up trash. I jump up as fast as I can, knocking my chair over in the process. Out of the corner of my eye as I pass, I notice the red light of the camera. Still recording. Thank God. I peak my head out into the living room and see Jameson and Scarlett hugging and giggling.

"Jameson, get in here, please." I plead.

"No, Parker," he says, "I was just about to get my phone."

"Jay." I say my voice breaking a little bit.

"Fine, what is it?" Jameson says, as he and Scarlett follow me back into the studio. Hayden has tears falling out of her eyes as she hands Jameson the picture she had removed from the monkey. It was a photo of Jameson's younger sister, Ana.

"What's this?" Jameson says while his hands start to shake. As Jameson is standing in front of me, I can see there's writing on the back of his picture. I grab it out of his hand, assemble all three, flip them over, and stare.

COME FIND ME :)

OR ELSE </3

72 HOURS

"This sick asshole!" Hayden yells through her tears. "What do we do now, guys?! My parents literally don't deserve this. My mom has already been through so much."

Jameson grabs me by the shoulders and starts to shake me back into my brain. I can feel panic down to my fingertips, but I know I have to stay calm for the sake of everyone else. I got us into this mess. I know Hayden loves her parents more than anything. They were the best and most supportive white-picket fence parents a lot of us in our late twenties weren't that fortunate to have. I also know how much Jameson loves Ana, also. They were inseparable when the two of them lived in Texas years ago. He's so proud of the person she's becoming. Plus, her life is just starting. She just finished college. I can feel the tears well up in my eyes as the thought of my grandma passes through. My grandma is literally my biggest rock and supporter in my whole life. She can make me laugh when I feel my worst. She helped raise me through teenage parents and taught me how to be the person I am today through my depression, anxiety, and gender issues.

"Parker!" I start to pay attention to Jameson yelling and shaking me. "Show me everything you know about Whitcom Industries right now!" He shoves the computer in my face.

All I can muster is a shaky "Okay," and I start typing in whitcomindustries.com, where before I had seen a nicely designed landing page featuring doctors and other important-looking people in lab coats. The page had been filled with links to all the different new technologies that were "Coming Soon" with associated contact numbers and emails listed. Now, after my right pinky finger clicks the Enter key, what pops up on the search bar is only a 404 error message. I try again, thinking I must've spelled something wrong, but the same thing pops up over and over again.

"Guys, I promise I looked up Whitcom before accepting their payment. I'm seriously not that dumb. It was here, a whole website with tech and doctors and contact information. I literally have no idea what's going on."

"You said you didn't even know what kind of company Whitcom Industries even was, Parker!" Hayden says, scolding me.

I sigh and say, "I looked up their website, of course. I said maybe they're the company that's behind Spirit Halloween because I wanted to be more light-hearted to you guys and not scare you as much. I didn't really think it was important to say their website looked all fancy. I'm sorry, I didn't even look at their About Me tab. Come to think of it, I didn't even press the drop-down button. I'm sorry, guys, I was just so excited to get the money and the box."

Everyone goes dead silent for the first time since we began. Their private opinions of me and the box were clearly on all their minds.

I click over to my email, type in my password, and try to find the contact email that had previously connected me with Whitcom Industries. No email found. For a split second, I think I'm losing my mind.

"He must have erased everything, don't you guys think? Maybe there was no Whitcom Industries at all," Scarlett quietly peeps.

I had honestly forgotten she was even in the room.

"What are you even still doing here?" Hayden yells.

"I'm sorry, I was just trying to help." Scarlett looks down at her feet and walks out of the room.

"Nice one, Hayden," Jameson says, as he follows her out of the room. I look at Hayden and give her a little squeeze on the leg as her tears start flowing more and more.

"Hey Scarlett, I didn't mean it, I'm just really, really worried about my parents. I'm glad you're trying to help. It's more than any other person you just met would do," Hayden chokes out.

Jameson and Scarlett come back in the room while Scarlett gives Hayden a little hug as if to say it's all okay.

"We have to go find him. We have to do what we're told or else... I mean literally, *or else,*" I say to the group, who are all still staring at the note on the back of our families' pictures.

"I hate to admit it, but you're right, Parker. We can't go to the cops now. Prank or not, our loved ones are in danger, and the only way they're going to be safe is if we go." Jameson says.

"We have three days, according to the note. We were going to film on Friday, so I know we're all free. Let's go then. It gives us a whole day to get stuff ready for potentially waltzing into a murder house. We need weapons, rope, gloves, masks and whatever else you guys can think of," I say as I turn to Hayden. "Baby, if they're going to play by the rules they set, your parents are going to be fine, okay? There's no reason to worry about them right now. Don't call them, either. You'll just freak them out, and we might lose this opportunity to save them. I love you."

Hayden looks me in the eyes and nods. She silently mouths "I love you, too."

"Let's all just take it in right now. None of us are in the right mindsets to make any choices, okay? Jameson, I'll call you tomorrow, and we can make a list and a plan," I say.

Jameson agrees, looks over at Scarlett and says, "Will you stay the night with me? I promise, nothing like that. I just think I need someone."

"Of course," Scarlett says. "We'll talk to you guys tomorrow. I'm here for you guys, and I know it's weird, but I feel like I'm in this too, now."

We all look at each other deep in the eyes and nod. Jameson and Scarlett head out the front door without another word.

Hayden has been a mess all night, and I can't blame her. I have been, too. Growing up in a household like Hayden's, you were allowed to show emotions. I guess I was too embarrassed or too stubborn to show mine, so I've always had this mask in my back pocket to be able to obscure my emotions at a moment's notice. I'm trying to be strong for her, but all I can think to say is that it's all going to be okay, even though I know I'm lying through my teeth. Deep down, Hayden knows this, too. We lay in bed with her head on my chest. I finally feel the tears stop falling and can hear her shallow breaths deepen, and she starts twitching in her sleep. I hope and pray to whomever is up in the sky that the girl of my dreams gets to have sweet dreams tonight. Boba also knows there's something wrong and won't leave her side. I can hear his slight snores through her arms.

It's 1:26 a.m.

It's freezing outside.

I hear Michacl yell, "Come on, Parker, we gotta go in before we wake anyone up with our flashlights."

For a moment, I'm confused that my childhood best friend is beckoning me this way, but what I see in front of me is the old St. James Hospital that's been closed for 55 years. When I walk over to him, I can feel the weight on my chest, and I know I'm 18 again. Cole was also there, but he was never too far behind, anyway. We cut the wire to the fence separating the back courtyard of the hospital from the alley.

The only entrance we could see is a small window and, at the bottom of the window, there was a 15-foot drop for the drainage of any water that might accumulate after the snow melted in the summer. It felt like the dead of winter, but as we know, there are only two seasons in Montana, and it could just as well have been late spring. The railing that blocked off the drop was completely covered in a blanket of slick ice, and so was the concrete around the window. We all, as quietly as possible, dragged each other by the puffy coats on our back off of the ice and through the window to the first floor of the abandoned hospital.

Everyone stayed quiet as we passed the rat-shit infested floors. Once we got past the small hallway, the building opened up to a magnificent rotunda with tiles on the ground that looked like an art piece. Looking around at the broken chandeliers and stretchers, to the right of the broken-down elevator was a trail of blood. This trail of blood looked as if the bleeding someone had been dragged around the corner while gripping at anything they could. I've been here before, but I never had the guts to follow the blood.

Everything's on the line now.

I'm going to follow it now.

I need to follow it now.

So I will.

So I am.

Suddenly, I looked back. I saw that I was alone. Michael and Cole had gone. I had a strange feeling that they had never been there in the first place. I walked on. The blood had become thick and wet, fresh here. Once I turned the corner, I stopped short. I stood, frozen to the spot in horror at the scene before me.

There was my grandma, hanging by a noose, with her left ear completely cut off. She had been stripped naked, her side had been roughly cut and poorly stapled back together, and she was barely standing on a plastic bucket. She reached for me, but her eyes were fixed on a spot somewhere behind me. I implicitly realized she wasn't reaching out for my help, but warning me.

Before I could turn around and meet my fate, I wake up in my bedroom in a cold sweat and with a panic attack. I'm vaguely aware of Hayden tugging on my shirt, but she is still asleep. I lie there with my small family in my arms, telling myself over and over again that it was only a dream, *only* a dream, only a dream.

Chapter 4

I wake in the morning at 6:30, early as usual. Still sleepy and puffy-eyed, I feel like when one of your loved ones dies and you forget for a split second upon waking. I stumble over to make myself a cup of "homemade" coffee with my Keurig. The aroma of the coffee brewing mixed with the stench of the organs still on my counter oozing through the tight plastic bags we tried to shove them in gave me a jolt. I felt my heart fall to the pit of my stomach and the acid bubbling up my throat. "Dammit," I whisper to myself, remembering the shitshow we are attending.

Ever since I was a kid, TV would be my savior. Whenever I was having a small meltdown or a depressive episode, I would turn on the TV and be taken away to another world–a world in which I wasn't living, a world where every impactful moment pulled the strings on the butterfly effect of the future. I always sat in front of the TV and wanted to be the hero on the screen, but I don't think they ever showed the fears of the hero very well anymore. I may or may not be the hero of this fucked up story, but damn–if you know sheer fear, that's all I felt while I reached for my oat milk creamer, poured some in and clumsily stirred with a fork. Feeling too nauseous to drink my barista masterpiece, I sit on the couch and grab my laptop. Hayden and Boba are still sleeping soundly, and they will be for another hour or two.

Speaking of TV, one of my favorite reality shows is *Catfish*. After eight seasons, fake or not, I've learned how to use a computer to reverse search and find anything that I want to find. This morning, I'm desperate to find anything on Whitcom Industries, so I start digging. Going back to whitcomindustries.com still gives the 404 error. I try some Googling. Neither Whitcom Industries nor this place appear to exist.

I hop onto my money app where I received the payment, and there's no transaction showing at all. It may as well have never occurred to look at the app.

I can't do anything to trace back the mystery box because they hired someone to get it for us–or, on the other hand, obviously sent it to us themselves.

The next thing I do is Google Map the longitude and latitude coordinates from the box. Just like last night, it pings in the north downtown Denver area. I keep zooming and zooming hoping to see the house, but there's nothing there. Just train tracks, like Scarlett said.

Seeing as Google Maps updated fewer than 4 days ago, there's no way the house could have been demolished in that amount of time. The tiniest shard of hope that this is just a huge–and effective–prank piercing my heart, I text my grandma and just say "Hi."

I sit in silence for a minute until I hear my phone buzz back at me.

The text says "Hi, sweetheart! How are you?" I sigh in relief from knowing she's at home, probably eating her morning donuts and Coca Cola.

I hear the shower turn on in our master bedroom.

It's pretty weird that Hayden didn't come out and say "Good morning, baby!", but I should give her a break. She's freaked out. I get up and head in the bathroom through the unlocked door.

"Can I join you?" I say over the sound of running water and splashing.

Hayden just barely peeps out a "Yes."

We spend the next 20 minutes in the shower, reassuring each other and wiping away tears. We needed that; we needed that time together before going to this house. Once we get out of the shower, we get ready for the day in silence. Once clothes are on and teeth are brushed, Hayden gets Boba and sits on the couch with her with the Notes app open on her phone.

"Okay," she says, "Let's get serious, Parker. No more tears, they're not going to do us any good anymore."

We lace up our shoes, leash up Boba and head to the nearest hardware store.

"I think we should split up and grab the stuff we need." Hayden says.

I shake my head and say, "Okay, but tomorrow, there's not one moment we aren't together. I've seen too many horror movies to split up from you."

Hayden agrees, and we go our separate ways in Home Depot. Just thinking back to all the stupid ghost hunting expeditions my friends and I would undertake (and thanks to my sweet dream), I know I need gloves and, potentially, some rope. I stumble on some black gloves immediately and throw them in my basket. I then stop by the pocket knife section and grab a multitool with two very sharp knives, around 4 inches each.

I think back to all the times in my life where I would walk into a party or even a restaurant and people would think I was ready to fight. It must be the way I walk with my hands always in a fist or the way I can't breathe through my nose really well so I have a weird scowl across my eyebrows.

What most people soon come to realize is that I literally cannot hurt a fly. *What the hell am I doing?* My heart starts beating at a rapid pace, and my hands start to shake as it all finally hits me. *I literally got everyone I love in my life involved with a murderer. How the fuck did this happen?*

I start to gasp for air in aisle four, my hands clutching my chest as I lean into the metal shelves holding all the multitools. All I can picture is everyone dying and I'm left alone. So alone in my apartment, staring at the walls. Not feeling a fucking thing.

Is this selfish? I wonder, imagining what would happen to me if everyone else was gone. I start to sweat, but my skin feels ice cold at the same time.

All this because my stupid bands never made it. I always wanted to be a household name; now look where we are.

I internally begin to scream at myself.

YOU'RE AT HOME DEPOT GETTING TOOLS TO GO SEARCH A MURDERER'S HOUSE WITH YOUR BEST FRIEND AND THE LOVE OF YOUR LIFE, YOU STUPID IDIOT. YOU SHOULD'VE JUST STAYED AND DELIVERED PIZZA NOW YOUR GRANDMA–

I feel a hand on my shoulder. It's Hayden, shaking me and saying, "Baby, it's okay, you're just having a panic attack. It's going to be okay."

I open my eyes and realize I'm on the floor of aisle four with an audience surrounding me. I finally take a deep breath and stand up.

"They're okay, everyone. Nothing to see here," Hayden says, shooing them away.

"I'm really sorry, Hayden," I start to explain as the shame builds up.

She knows that I hate being weak and that I hate other people seeing me in these weak moments.

"Shhh. Don't be. I got everything I need, let's head to the checkout." Hayden says while she takes my hand and leads me to the front of the store.

Once we get to the checkout, it occurs to me that it looks like we're the ones doing the murdering.

Hayden had taken full advantage of the store and throws two flashlights, a pack of pens, a notebook, walkie-talkies, batteries, one hammer, one screwdriver, a set of lockpicks, the multi-tool and a first-aid kit onto the counter.

I follow and toss my four pairs of gloves and length of rope up to the lady checking us out. Maybe the fear of looking like a murderer with all this stuff was only in my head, because the lady at the checkout didn't seem to think anything of it, just finished ringing us up, and we start to leave the store.

Hayden and I begin our walk outside to the car and, before I know it, I'm grabbed by a lady with ratty hair and torn-up clothes. Even though she looks homeless, she smells immaculate. Like fresh roses and eucalyptus candles. My first thought is that this is Denver, she's probably just on the side of the store begging for money, but she seems different.

She grabs both of my shoulders and starts to shake me, yelling, "She's coming. She's tired of war. She wants you!"

I just stand there, too stunned to actually free myself. As usual, my savior, Hayden, tries to get in between us.

"What the hell are you on, lady? Let them go!" Hayden shouts.

The lady drops her arms to her sides, eyes rolling into the back of her head, and says, "She wants you too, beautiful. She wants everyone."

Heads of passersby start to turn to us, as if we're the ones making a scene. I already made a scene in the store, they're probably thinking, so what's so different outside?

The lady then smiles and says in the sweetest, most polite tone possible, "You two have a great day," and starts to walk off.

"What the fuck is with today?" Hayden says. I let out a fake laugh, but deep down, I'm more disturbed than I've ever been.

We get to the car, get in, and just stare at the dashboard together, wondering what to do next. I mean, there's no manual telling you what to do with the rest of your day before you go hunt down the person blackmailing you.

Even though we both feel nauseous, I insist that we grab something to eat on the way home to keep our strength up. We cruise through the McDonald's drive through and both order some nuggets. Even Boba got a nugget himself.

I look at how happy he is in the back seat while Hayden gives him a nugget dipped in Ranch. That little shit has no idea what's going on. He's just living his life, waiting for his next meal or walk. I wish life was that simple sometimes.

Fuck, I wish life was that simple all the time. I don't understand how waking up to dinosaur oatmeal and Pokémon on my Grandma's TV one moment turned into me trying to make a living and being an adult the next.

I need to stop complaining to myself. I need to be in the right mindset and be strong for Hayden.

We get back to the house, and Hayden says, "We need to make a plan if things go wrong."

"I agree," I say, even though making plans has never been my strong suit. Hayden gets one of her new pens and her notebook out and starts writing down notes.

"So, if we do come across the people we saw in the photos or we find other people, we're going to save them, right?" Hayden asks.

"I mean…" I pause and think. "Yes, we will for sure try and help them, but we have to first find out what this guy wants before we go in and try and be The Amazing Spider-Man, you know?"

Hayden nods and starts planning out the most minuscule things. I love her so much, but right now my brain cannot handle what she's trying to plan. We have no idea what we're actually getting into, there's no planning for this. The house doesn't even exist on Google Maps. There's no way to make a plan. I sit there and try to be supportive as best as I can.

Hayden finally taps out of the planning at around three in the afternoon and puts on a reality show, just how we like to drown out the real world. I check my phone and see that I have a message from Jameson.

Jay: Did you guys go to the store? Are you all ready for tomorrow?

Me: Yes, Hayden got some smart stuff. Let's meet at 12, my house?

Jay: Yeah, that sounds good dude. It's still okay if Scarlett comes with us, right?

Me: For sure, if it makes you feel more comfortable you whipped asshat ;)

Jay: Shut up dude. She's been so supportive and today, she hasn't even left.

Me: Alright dude I would say be careful, but you know we're going to a murder house tomorrow.

Jay: We got this; I mean we have to.

Me: I'll see ya tomorrow at 12. Call me to buzz you in.

Jay: You got it fuck face sleep tight.

If only he knew how I actually slept.

Later, we end up putting on the new *Vacation* movie to try and get our minds off the following day. I can feel the anxiety swelling up inside my veins. My legs won't stop twitching, and it annoys Hayden to the point where she moves to the other side of the couch.

I know a lot about Hayden's childhood, and it seems like she's the kind of person that doesn't really know what anxiety or depression is, especially when they reach breaking point. Of course she's been sad before in her life, and has probably worried about things, but it's never been a big deal. When I've talked about my struggles, it seems to always surprise her to the point of not understanding what I'm actually going through.

I mean, fuck, I wish I could even describe correctly what my head is ever thinking. I can hear her giggling at the movie beside me on the couch like nothing in the world is wrong. I'm beyond happy that she can put this out of her head, even if only for the span of a two-hour movie. Me, on the other hand–I'm staring at a spot on the wall right below the TV thinking of every possible outcome that could happen. I know it's not healthy, but that's just the way I've grown up trying to process extreme feelings. I take 20 mg of Lexapro to try and counteract it, but things like this that light the fuse make it almost impossible to handle.

Time moves on fast-forward, and I soon find myself staring at the credits and realizing I don't know a single thing that happened in the movie. I turn to Hayden and see she's fast asleep on the corner of the couch with Boba at her feet. I sit up, turn off the tv, and put my head in my hands and start to rub my temples. All of a sudden, I hear a rock hit my window. My first thought is Hayden's locked out and forgot the FOB to the main door. This has happened to both of us a handful of times, and if you're home alone, you're screwed until the other one makes it back home or you go and bug the downstairs neighbors that are somehow never the same people. I stare at the window and another small rock hits it hard, this time waking up Hayden.

"What's happening? What's that noise?" Hayden says, yawning. A third rock hits hard enough that I'm surprised when the window doesn't break. I get up and head to the porch.

"It's probably just some dumb kids, I'll go tell them I'll call the police on them." I say.

I head to the porch and Hayden follows. We open the door and both rest our arms over the railing.

What we see is a man standing in the middle of the road, faintly illuminated by the street lights. He looks tall and lanky with normal black ripped jeans and a dark-colored hoodie on with the hood up. He was just standing there, staring at us on the balcony. I see him drop the rock from his hand.

"Hey! You! What the fuck is wrong with you? Stop throwing rocks at my apartment!" I yell out into the cold air.

"Parker, don't make a scene." Hayden says, rubbing my back. Boba runs outside to join us and looks through the metal bars of our balcony with a concerned look on his face. The man says nothing and continues to stare.

"I mean, what should we do, baby? He's obviously not leaving." I say, annoyed.

"I feel like we're having a damn staring competition, and what if he starts throwing stuff at us or pulls out something way worse, like a gun?"

All of a sudden, the man raises his hand and points to the sky.

I look up to the stars and see nothing.

I was kind of hoping he was showing us aliens or something. I mean, after this week, it wouldn't surprise me. Maybe they would even save us from whatever's about to happen tomorrow.

Hayden sees me look to the sky and says, "He's not pointing up. He's saying '1'. As in one more day. That's all."

She's right. We have 24 more hours to come find him or else who knows what will happen to our loved ones.

"Is that him?" I whisper.

Suddenly a white pick-up truck barrels down the street, screeching all the way, and runs right over the man in the black hoodie.

"OH MY GOD!" Hayden yells as her face hides into my shoulder.

I have no clue how to react as the white truck slams on his breaks as the man lies in the street, lifeless. The truck driver appears to have no idea what to do and drives off as fast as he can. I stare in complete shock at the dead man on the street, one moment threatening our lives and the next lying broken on the white paint that splits the road.

"What the fuck," I stammer as Hayden takes her head off my shoulder and looks over the balcony one last time.

The man, somehow, is starting to stand up. His right leg is bent, broken at the tibia, and his left drags behind him. His arms look all wrong, like the subject of a game of hangman after you've failed to guess the correct word. Blood wraps the street like a Christmas present, but the man seemed like he didn't have a care in the world. He limps off the street without a word, bones cracking with each step and blood dripping into the street. He disappears into the night.

Chapter 5

It's Friday. Hayden and I have been pretty quiet all morning. We have no idea how to comfort each other or ourselves. After last night, our nervous systems were both in shock. We finally found sleep and let the night take us all the way until 10 a.m., which is very unusual for me. Both too nauseous to eat, I make us both force down at least one granola bar for energy. My phone starts ringing right at noon.

It's Jameson on the other end, saying, "Let me innnnnnnnnn," in the most girlish tone possible. I don't say a word and buzz them upstairs. Jameson opens the door first and I can hear him say, "Ladies first." He always was one to use gendered terms more than anyone I know. It was almost impossible for him to start calling me by my preferred pronouns, but eventually he got it. He just had to start calling everyone in his life they/them to perfect it. It meant a lot to me, my best friend trying to make me happy after growing up the way he did in Texas.

They finally get through the door giggling, and take in the doom and gloom that make up Hayden and I.

"Hey guys! Why is the mood so low in here? I know were going to a murder house and, like, everyone we love might die, but, like, we all can't be a team with this attitude," Jameson jokes.

I can see Scarlett elbow him in the ribs to say in her own way to give us a break.

"Sit down for a second," I say, and I begin to tell Jameson and Scarlett what had happened last night. For the first time in the last couple days, I finally saw Scarlett show signs of worry. Her hand is over her mouth to try and stifle her gasp at the fact the man was run over by a car. She hasn't said much, but I can tell she was super uncomfortable with the facts that I was giving them.

"Damn, guys. That's really intense. Nothing happened over at my house," Jameson said in an apologetic tone.

"Yeah, well. Let's just start heading over there, right? We got our warning. Might as well get there before it gets dark and even more creepy," I say. "You guys ready?"

Jameson looks at Scarlett and nods, but then Jameson says, "Let's go over the plan first."

We spend the next hour or so going over the plan and what we'll do if something truly awful happens. We have our walkie-talkies, and our plan is very concrete in terms of not splitting up. Everyone has ideas except Scarlett. I take it as her not wanting to jump in the middle of three best friends', with literal blood on the line, plans.

It seems like Scarlett snapped out of her head after an awkward dread-filled silence after planning and yells, "Let's go! Race you back downstairs, Jay!" giving him a kiss on the cheek and rushing to the door.

"All our stuff is downstairs, anyways. We will see you down there!" Jameson giggles and runs out the door.

I look over at Hayden, who hasn't said a word in hours. She has her arms crossed and one leg over the other. It's the kind of look I get when I forget to do the dishes or feed Boba.

"What the fuck was that?" Hayden says uncrossing her arms and pointing in the direction of Jameson and Scarlett. "I mean, Scarlett has no place in all of this, and the way she acted when you were describing what happened last night? It feels like she thinks this is just a giant game we're playing. Jameson just met this girl, for God's sake, and now she's our partner in crime?"

"I think she was just worried about the guy that came to our house last night. I mean, wouldn't that kind of freak you out if you heard that story?" I say, trying to comfort Hayden.

"No, Parker," Hayden says, "She wasn't holding her hand over her mouth because she was worried, she was laughing. I could see from my angle she was fucking laughing."

"Okay, I believe you, but just know you're under a lot of stress right now and probably in shock. You can't be sure she was laughing; all I saw was she was upset about last night. But baby, I don't want to fight. I think Jameson needs her like I need you. Once we get there and see what's up, we can tell her to leave or something, okay? But right now, she knows everything. We can't just let her loose," I say. "Whatever, Parker, let's just get downstairs and get this over with." Hayden says, annoyed. I sigh, get my backpack, lock the door and follow Hayden down to my car.

Jameson sees us and yells, "You're driving!"

Like I didn't already know that. I'm usually the chauffeur for our whole friend group, even though I'm usually the one that ends up drinking too much and the one who has to worry about getting my hungover ass up to go back downtown and find my car the next morning.

I unlock the car and everyone shoves their backpacks and gear into the back of my Jeep Compass. I hope that Jameson remembered to bring the attachable Go Pro cameras, because I'm not wasting one minute not getting everything on camera.

Maybe this is the documentary that'll get me off the ground and my feet into the latest Tesla, I think.

Jameson starts talking, knocking me out of my dream-car daydreams, and says, "Hey, guys, before we go, I just want to let you guys in on something that I found."

All of us are very curious. We huddle around Jameson and a weird book he had just placed on the hood of my car.

He continues, "So yesterday, when Scarlett left my house for a little bit, I got really bored of playing Call of Duty so I decided to actually do some digging. I figured you already tried to look up more about Whitcom Industries and stuff, but I was more intrigued by another object in the mystery box that we didn't talk about that much."

"Okay, get to it, Jay," I say, antsy to get on the road.

"Well, we never really talked about that weird symbol we found carved into the box, so I started to do some research. I first started trying to describe it to Google, but all that really came up was Legend of Zelda references until I almost gave up out of frustration and pressed the 'I'm feeling lucky' button. It brought me to the Denver Library website that stated they had a whole section just dedicated to demons and spirits. After doing a little bit of searching, I mean guys, this place is huge–"

Hayden and I roll our eyes because we know this is definitely the first time Jameson has ever been in a library. I laugh a little because he's acting like he's a little kid that found a candy shop for the first time. I've never even seen Jameson read a book besides Playboys on tour.

Jameson sees me laughing and finally says, "Shut up and listen! I found this book," and he pats the cover of the book on my car. The title reads *Pendants of the Occult.*

"I found the logo, the one that was carved into the box," Jameson flips to a dog-eared page and starts reading to us.

"'This pendant is carved, painted, drawn, or etched in skin to summon the demon Azazela, ruler of mind control. Azazela is known to have taught man to make weapons of war in the dark ages. In the 1990s, a cult tied to Azazela was at its all-time high of 46 members across Washington. They were known to try and summon this demon to enlist her help to take over the world. After three years of the cult spreading out over the Evergreen area, multiple members were later found dead, and most went missing. The two triangles are known to represent people on opposite sides having their own free will, but the 'x' going through both triangles leads to the thought of a person having their free will taken away and being condemned to the demon with mind control.'"

"Alright, I thought we were just dealing with a psychopath, but now we have literal demons involved?" Hayden says in a snarky tone.

I can tell deep down inside she's terrified like the rest of us, but she's never going to admit it to Jameson and Scarlett.

"That's definitely not all, guys," Jameson says as he pulls out his laptop. "I Googled that farm in Washington, and guess what the name of it was?"

We all shrug and urge Jameson to just tell us without all the theatrics.

"It was called Whitmore and Compton's Family Farms. Don't you get it, guys? This creepy ass dude put his and his friends' names together to make Whitcom Industries!"

"Holy shit, Jameson, nice detective work! What else did you find on him?" I say, my bones wanting to jump out of my skin with joy because we found something that might help us with this ordeal.

"That's the shitty part. Other than the farm and a paragraph in this demon book, this guy is a ghost. No socials, no criminal record, literally nada," he says. "I even tried to find members tied to the cult, but it just comes up with so many people missing in Washington, from Native Americans to people saying they were abducted by aliens, Bigfoot, you freaking name it, it's a giant forest of missing people."

"You did all of this without me?" Scarlett says, and I glance over in her direction and see her face is drained of blood. I can also see that she's been picking at her thumbs through this entire conversation, making them bleed.

"Well yeah, babe, like I said, I got really bored and thought I would try and help out with this situation," Jameson says, trying to comfort her, while I see Hayden roll her eyes.

"Okay, can we just get going?" Scarlett says, trying to urge us to get into the car. She opens the door to the back seat and sits down. Jameson follows her and shuts the door.

"This is awkward and weird and she shouldn't be here," Hayden says.

"Right, I have no idea what that was about! Do you think she's just mad at Jameson that she wasn't involved in his search?" I say to Hayden as we are lean on the hood of my Jeep.

"Parker, like I said, I don't have a good gut feeling about this girl. Whether she's just being a primadonna or not, I don't like it." Hayden says quietly.

I can see Jameson rubbing Scarlett's back in the back of my car while her arms are crossed. I can imagine Jameson is trying to make a joke just to make her smile, and it must be working, as I can see her opening up to him again.

"You know I can't deal with confrontation, Hayden. I can't just tell my best friend, 'hey, sorry, the only thing that's kind of keeping you sane right now and not thinking about how your sister is going to die is here but like Hayden and I have a really bad feeling about her so she should get an Uber and go home,'" I say to Hayden, and then automatically follow it with, "Sorry, baby, I don't mean to be an ass. I literally just don't know what to do."

Hayden sighs and comes over to me for a huge hug that I wasn't expecting. She says in my ear, "I don't expect you to do that, I'm sorry too. Can we please just keep an eye on her? I love you so much and believe we're going to get through this together. We can't start a fight for the 20-minute drive to downtown," I smile and squeeze her back, not really knowing when I will get another hug like this. Probably when all this shit is behind us.

The drive into the arts district of Denver was oddly quiet. Usually, us three are blasting the latest Spotify playlist of the year that we all contribute to or singing along to early 2000s pop music. This ride, on the other hand, has all our heads in another world. Mine was wondering how the hell this night is going to unfold and about the mystery between Whitmore and Compton farms.

This is the trek I used to drive every day on my way to my dead-end job before we started Put Up or Shut Up. The leaves are starting to change colors in the most beautiful way. I never really understood how much people loved fall. Fall back home was cold and the leaves all died in a day. You didn't get to see the concrete on the ground until the next summer. But here, here you get to see the leaves change and feel that tiny chill in the air that always comes after my birthday. Here we are again, my mind trying to help me hide from the dangers that present themselves by thinking of fall. Thinking of Hayden and I at the beginning of fall on our coffee dates, her in my extra-large hoodies, and, most of all, us cuddling up on the couch watching horror movies. Now we're in our own horror movie, and I gotta say, it's nothing like you could ever imagine.

When we finally arrive north of downtown, Jameson pulls out the map on his phone.

"Parker, we're really close. It looks like there could be a car entrance somewhere around these train tracks."

We pass all of the breweries and businesses on the street and hit the train tracks. I continue to drive up and down the street looking for a way to get between the tracks and the local businesses on the other side of the bridge.

I begin to get frustrated and say, "Dude, you gotta help me. I have no idea where the hell to drive this car."

Jameson is frantically scrolling on his phone, trying the best he can to be a good navigator.

"Maybe we should just park and walk over the train tracks, man. I mean at least while it's still light outside," Jameson says.

I ended up parking where you would park if the Rockies ever won a playoff game and continued to play into October, but for right now, the lot was empty besides a few cars here and there.

Hayden turns around in the car and says, "Alright, guys. Let's grab our stuff and start walking. We got this, we're a team! Let's go meet this guy and save our loved ones!"

"Nice pep talk babe, let's go!" I say, trying to get everyone to high five me.

We start walking over the tracks. There are no trains in sight. I mean, on a Friday after work hours, I wouldn't expect anything to be rolling around these tracks but parked cabooses.

We walk for what feels like forever, and the afternoon is stretching into 6 p.m. The sun is starting to set, and it's getting harder to look for oncoming trains. We keep jumping track after track. Jameson swears that it's right up ahead, but the map on his phone keeps changing paths because we aren't on any known path whatsoever.

All of a sudden, we can feel the tracks start to rumble. We're pinned between two parked trains with nowhere to go. It's the Denver light rail coming right towards us.

"Sprint to your right!" Scarlett, of all people, yells at everyone.

We start running as fast as we can, trying to outrun the light rail. We finally make it to the end of an abandoned caboose on another track and dive right in front of it before the light rail sliced through our skin and bones. We all start getting up and brushing the dirt off ourselves. Obviously trying to make light of the situation of almost getting hit by the Denver light rail, I say, "Well geez, that was a close one, guys!"

No one responds to me. They're all looking straight forward in awe.

There it is. A blue house, just like the pictures in the mystery box. There are no cars out front and no lights. The windows are boarded up, and the paint on the porch is chipping. There are no neighbors in sight. It's like this person bought this house before Denver was even a city. They must have begged them and bribed them with money, but it was their property, and they didn't move. I kept wondering how anyone got to this house without jumping all the train tracks.

Right now, there is no forward escape route. Tracks and trains are blocking our way to the skyscrapers. It feels like we're trapped in a board game maze. I don't feel lucky enough to roll the dice for the right numbers, and I think everyone is realizing that.

"Okay, guys," I say, trying to be the leader and holding my own God complex close to my heart. "We're prepared. Let's just go and see if the doors open and what the inside holds for us if it does."

Everyone nods, and we all start walking up to the house.

Jameson starts to unzip his backpack reaching for the cameras I was relieved to see he remembered.

"Okay, guys, everyone gets one. The straps are extra stretchy, but they will all fit snug and the camera will rest on your chest, hopefully barely noticeable." Jameson says as he starts to string the cameras around each person's body.

"Alright," he says with one last tug on his straps, "Let's get this over with."

Everyone presses the top of the Go Pros all at once and, yet again, I can see the red record light starring me in the face. It feels like a lifetime ago that we were making the opening video to the mystery box. The demonic symbol of Azazela was carved into the porch where the three people were sitting in the photo. It's gigantic, covering the entire porch all the way up to the front door.

"I need a second. Jameson, will you stay here with me just for a minute? Maybe you two should go in there and check it out and we will keep watch from out here, and if anything happens, we can notify each other with the walkie talkies," Scarlett says.

"What? No. The plan was to stick together!" Hayden yells. "Honestly, Scarlett, you don't have anything on the line here. We need to get in and get this over with."

"Stop it, Hayden!" Jameson says. "Look, Scarlett may have a point. We need to scope out the outside, too, and she's scared, okay? Let the girl have some emotions. We are all scared."

"This is ridiculous, don't you care about your sister?" Hayden spits back at Jameson.

"Don't you fucking say another word about her! Yes, I care, that's why I'm here, aren't I?" Jameson starts yelling back.

"Okay, okay, okay, stop it, you two! Jameson, go take Scarlett around the house and have her take a breather. I guess we can split up for now, but keep your walkie on. Let's go Hayden, we got this." I say as Hayden takes the walkie out of her backpack and shoves it at Jameson's chest.

Jameson and Scarlett walk back down the porch stairs and I can hear her apologizing to Jameson quietly as tears fall down her face. I've honestly never seen Jameson this into someone, but I have to let it go because he stuck by my side through everything I've gone through.

"I guess I'll just try the door?" I say, as I can see Hayden shaking out of pure adrenaline and fear.

"Just you and me forever?" Hayden whispers.

"Forever and more, baby," I say, and try to put on the best smile I can, even though I can feel it come off weakly. I reach for the door, so splintered and fragile one shove and it feels like it would turn to saw dust and, not to our surprise, it opens with a welcoming creak.

CHAPTER 6

Hayden and I hold hands as the door swings open. At first glance, you would probably think this is just a regular house–open concept with a dining room to the left and the living room to the right once you walk in. Beyond the left-hand side dining room, there's an open kitchen with old wooden cabinets and white appliances.

The first thing that really caught my eye during my initial once-over: to the right side of the house, where one would think one would see a nice couch with a big-screen TV, maybe movies on a wall shelf with some family photos, but that, of course, was not the case for the murder house. The light blue carpet was stained with blood, with spots everywhere else. Not even straight bleach would stand a chance. The walls were bare and the popcorn ceiling was falling to pieces. On top of the bloody carpet, instead of a nice family couch or a Lazy Boy, there were four wooden pews like you would see in a church. They were chipped and falling apart, but the soft part where one kneels to pray was down and worn.

In front of the pews was a giant steel sculpture of the occult sign of Azazela.

Hayden and I both didn't say a word as we stared up at this gigantic statue. It's one thing to see a giant gory Crucifix at church, but you grow up with that, or at least I did. But when you see a giant representation of demon-worshiping mind control bullshit that's going on here, you definitely want to piss your pants.

"Hey guys, you alive?" buzzed the walkie talkie. Hayden and I drop each other's hands and both jump out of our skin like we've just experienced the greatest jump scare in cinematic history.

"God damn!" Hayden says, starting to laugh. I press the walkie and say to Jameson, "Yeah, we're alive, but you won't believe your eyes once you're in here. Over."

"Well, so far, all there is out here is a weird shed thing, nothing else. We're about to check that out and then I'll buzz you again. Over." Jameson says, sounding bored and a little jealous.

"Copy," I say into the walkie before handing it back to Hayden.

"Let's not touch anything yet, okay babe?" Hayden says to me, even though we've both put on our black gloves already. I nod and start heading toward the other room, which should be the dining room. On the wall, there are numbers–one through eight–with one lever with wire hanging from each. Four of those wires are connected to four hand pistols on a bar-like mechanism. The wires are so entangled, we couldn't tell which ones wrap around the trigger. The other four look as though they are going up into a tiny metal box below the guns. Who the hell knows what the fuck is in that little box?

The left handgun is pointing a tiny bit towards the left, and the one next to it is just pointing a tiny bit to the ground. The handgun on the right is also pointing just a little bit to the right, and the one next to that is pointing up. These may look like regular handguns, but the barrels all have multiple exits. From my uncle being so into guns when I was little (he even converted one of my grandmother's closets into a gun room), I know a sliver of information about them. These guns could have shells in them like a shot gun. That'll give you a nice spray of metal to your face. No matter where you stand in that room, a bullet or shards of a bullet are going to hit you.

Above the number is a rusty brown finger-painted message, in which I can only assume is blood: "Choose Wisely."

"Okay, babe, what the fuck is this, some sort of boobie trap?" I say to Hayden, trying to get her attention. She walks over from the gigantic statue shrine and looks at the mechanism in front of me.

"I mean, are we really trying to recreate the *Saw* movies here? Please, Parker, don't touch that. We're already playing a game with our loved ones, there's no need to play this one, too." Hayden says in a sickened tone.

"I honestly don't understand what's going on here, though. We are here. We came to this dude's house. So far, there's literally nothing here besides some freaky shit. This place honestly looks abandoned. Like, who would even live here, ya know?" I say to Hayden and myself, getting pretty frustrated with the fact nothing else is happening. I suppose I should prefer it that way, but it's a little anticlimactic.

"I guess we just keep looking, babe." Hayden says to me as she heads into the kitchen. If this house was anywhere else in Denver and not plastered with blood and demonic praise, I could picture myself buying this for Hayden and I. Very quaint and cute. It's not an over-the-top mansion and not underdeveloped. It reminds me of my grandma's house I grew up in when I was a kid. All it needs is a huge Christmas tree with tinsel and my grampa watching football in the corner of the couch.

I follow Hayden into the kitchen. Every cabinet was empty besides a few canned goods you would see people fight over in any zombie movie. Each drawer looked like it had been broken open and the kitchen sink was rusted over. The only thing that seemed out of place was the refrigerator. Even though it was older, as in not stainless steel, it was very white and clean. Someone has been taking care of this certain fridge.

"I'm scared to open it," Hayden says, "I feel like I was nose blind to the body parts out of the mystery box but I don't know if I can handle whatever is in that fridge."

"I have to open it. I really don't care if curiosity kills the cat," I say. I take a big breath in and hold it as I open the door to the fridge. Surprisingly, nothing smelled. It was clean and organized like any fridge would be if your mother was in charge of putting away the groceries. The only weird thing was a total lack of food in this fridge. From top to bottom, there were mason jars of every shape and size with a light green liquid in every one of them. I start to look closer and notice that in each one, there is a big toe and an ear floating around. Each jar is labeled: Zach D., Rose M., Tucker P., Dan R., Caitlin L., and so on. There are about 30 jars stacked up in the most meticulous way.

"You think these are his trophies? Like he's murdering these people and keeping their body parts preserved in jars?" Hayden whispers through her fingers she's using to cover the awestruck look on her face.

"I think so," I say as I start to pick one up to get a closer look.

"Parker, I thought we agreed not to touch anything," Hayden says fearfully. I ignore her, which I promise I don't usually do, but I needed to see the details of these so-called trophies. The one I grabbed was labeled Emily W. I could still see the looped earrings in the top of the cut-off ear. The amputation looked precisely done, like whoever did this did it with a surgical scalpel, not like the janky sawed-off ear in the mystery box. The big toe also had remnants of toenail polish. Light blue.

"At least none of our people are actually in here," I say, trying to make the situation somewhat light-hearted. Hayden ignores me and rounds the corner to the bathroom and bedroom. I keep staring at the fridge until eventually Hayden yells from the bedroom in a frustrated tone. I pass the back door on the way and peek out toward the shed in the far-left corner of the backyard. The window is dirty and I can't see Jameson or Scarlett. I wonder shortly to myself what they're doing out there for so long.

"I don't get it. There's nothing else here. What are we supposed to do, for God's sake? We come here to see something, gain some information, and there's no one here. No one is even fucking here! How're we supposed to save our families, Parker?"

I know she's not expecting an answer, so I head toward her in the bedroom instead, which is entirely empty besides a stained mattress on the floor. I silently reach for her hand, but she's on a mission to figure out what the rest of the house holds. She walks out and I follow her all the way to the right in this circular house. Immediately before we're back in at the front near the demonic shrine area, there is a plain white door with a note.

You found me.

Dare to go further?

Adrenaline pumping, I reach for the doorknob before Hayden can tell me to stop. The door is locked with a tiny keyhole begging me to unlock it.

"So, we found him," Hayden says staring at the note. "That's all it says. 'Come find me,' and we found him. So, everyone has to be safe right? I mean, what if this was a just a ploy and everything is actually fake and he's filming us to get off or something?"

"I don't know what to do, Hayden. We did play by the rules and the note pretty much says that we fucking found him. Maybe it means we won. Maybe it means we should go find Jay and have a group chat about it. I don't even know how to open this door, it needs a key," I say.

To my surprise Hayden reaches for the door and tries the knob to make sure it's actually locked and a ghost isn't going to pop out at us.

"Alright, let's see." Hayden says are she grabs the walkie talkie out of her pocket. "Earth to Jameson, where are you guys? We need to talk. Over."

We wait a minute for Jameson to respond until eventually Hayden presses the walkie talkie again and says, "Jameson, please come in. We need to talk, where are you? Over."

All of sudden, static blares through the walkie talkie as though the button is being held down on the other one, but no one is talking. Hayden tries to press the button again, but with the button pressed on the other walkie, our device couldn't work.

"It's like he was going to reply and instead just kept holding the button. That's weird, we promised we would stay in touch in case either one of us needed the other," I say, getting annoyed at my best friend. "I guess we can just head to the shed and see if they're still out there?" I ask Hayden, who agrees, and we both head out the front door.

I check my phone and realize that it's actually dead. Of course, another horror movie cliché. If I even mention it to Hayden, she's going to rip my face off for not being prepared. It's dark outside, so I know it's past seven. I'm annoyed and wondering why the hell Jameson didn't just come into the house if he was done with the shed, this place could be full of skin-walkers or God-knows-what. The dead grass and weeds crunch under my shoes as loud as my dad used to chew his food.

I call out, "Jameson, dude!" with no reply. We head around to the shed with our flashlights leading the way. Once we reach the shed, we immediately notice the closed door.

Hayden looks at me and says, "I swear to God, if he tries to fucking scare us with Scarlett, I'm going to murder him myself. JAMESON, STOP PLAYING AND COME OUT," Hayden's right, this isn't the time for fun and games, so I swing the door open, preparing to be startled and then annoyed when he inevitably pops out at us. It's immediately apparent that no one is inside the shed. There's straw littering the floor, a single tool bench, and a small motorcycle with flat tires, which probably hasn't seen the road in decades. As soon as I step inside, I kick something across the floor.

"What was that?" Hayden asks as we begin scouring the floor with our flashlight beams until I spot a syringe with the tip soaked in blood. Its contents are reminiscent of the liquid which filled the syringe from the mystery box.

"Do you think..." Hayden starts and then trails off.

"No, let's not even think like that. They probably headed back into the house to find us right when we went out the front door. I did see a back door, but didn't check to see if it was open or not. It's a straight shot from this shed." I say, trying to keep Hayden's hopes up that nothing happened to Jameson or Scarlett.

"So we'll head back inside and see if they tried to meet us," she says, agreeing to stay positive. As soon as we turn around to leave the shed, I notice that there in the corner is the walkie talkie. The antenna had been busted off and the buttons broken, like someone had thrown it at the wooden wall. With lumps in our throats, we head back to the house.

We try the back door only to find out that it's locked from the inside. We both jog to the front door, and I know both our hearts are beating out of our chests. We throw the front door open, no longer fearing anything that might be inside waiting for us. We just need to find our friend. The place is the same as it was 10 minutes ago, before we went outside. We start looping through the house over and over again.

"Jameson!"

"Jay!"

"Scarlett!"

"JAY!" Hayden and I are now screaming. I'm again passing the locked white door with the sign beckoning us forward again while pacing around in desperation, and that's when I see it.

Jameson's favorite watch he wore tonight was looped around the doorknob like a nice Christmas decoration.

"Hayden, come here!" I yell to her as I hear my voice getting choked up in my throat.

"Oh, my God."

She comes around from the kitchen to see the Rolex hanging from the door.

"We need to go down there," I say, starting to really panic now. I grab the knob and start rattling it back and forth as though the lock will give out and I'll be able to waltz downstairs to save my best friend. My heart is beating out of my chest. The devil on my shoulder is laughing hysterically, telling me we knew what we were getting into. How did I think we could come to a murder house without something happening to someone?

"Parker, let's step back and think. You're going to give yourself a panic attack," Hayden tugs at my shoulder to get me away from the door.

"How do we get down there? We need to figure it out, fucking now!" I say, now banging on the door. I stalk into the living room and then to the dining room, where I see the guns on the wall.

"This has to be it, baby. We have to figure out this puzzle," I say, my fingertips brushing the wires connected to the guns.

"No! You're not pulling any of those! You have no idea what the numbers even do or anything!" Hayden starts yelling and begging me to step away. I drown out all the noise. I feel like it's fourth and goal during the state championship. I look at the four guns. My brain is running wild with adrenaline, like I have one minute left in an escape room, but one that's life or death.

Okay, okay, okay, think, Parker, I'm telling myself. Four guns might mean four numbers. Then I realize everything comes back to that stupid box we bought. I look at my wrist and see the numbers 1, 6, 5, and a black blob.

"It's the numbers from the pictures," I say to Hayden. "While you guys were going to call the cops and talking about it, I looked through the rest of the pictures. There were four numbers, and I wrote them down on my wrist. Honestly, I forgot about them and now I'm cursing the genetics that passed my dad's sweaty hands down to me." Hayden grabs my arm and tries to make out the numbers.

"I think it's either a two or a seven. Not to state the obvious, but if you're wrong, you're going to die, Parker. I can't live if you die in this house. There's no way." Hayden starts to cry. I can see the hope leaving her eyes.

"I can't leave Jameson here! He's my best friend and he wouldn't leave me," I say, wiping away some of her tears. "Please go in the kitchen to make sure the bullets can't hit you if worse comes to worse. If my number is wrong and I'm gone, you have to try the other one and save Jameson. Please, Hayden. Hayden, please. Tell me you hear me?" I say to her, trying to make her look me in the eyes. She nods slightly and I push her lightly to the kitchen.

"I love you with all my heart, baby." I say as I walk back towards the guns. I grab number one with my left hand and place my right palm on the levers of the numbers six and five. I'm now staring down the barrels of all four pistols, their metallic odor so thick in my nose I feel like I'm tasting nickels in my mouth. Then it hits me: why would it be 5,6,7? It would just be too easy, but at the same time, my grampa comes into my head. He's playing craps in Vegas. He's winning and begging for sevens. I can hear the people around him cheering him on while he sips his Manhattans. While he throws his dice down on the table in my mind's eye, I take my whole right hand and put it on levers five, six and seven. Refusing to even count to three, I close my eyes and yank the levers down with all my strength.

CHAPTER 7

Jameson

The lights lining the hall are blinding, but in momma's room, the only light glows from the machine hooked up to her body and the TV in the corner that only plays boring adult shows. I never understood why the adults always want to watch real people on the TV and never cartoons. Cartoons are the best, especially Pokémon. Dad fumbles into the room with his hands full of fountain sodas and McDonald's bags. Momma is happy that we brought her food from somewhere that wasn't the hospital cafeteria, and my dad starts unpacking everything and setting up the little couches so we could all sit next to each other.

"What's Ana going to eat? What did she ask for?" five-year-old me asks my Momma.

"Oh sweetie, she doesn't eat food yet and she won't for a while. So, you can just enjoy your nuggets to yourself until she's old enough to steal them from you!" Momma says in a playful voice. After we were done eating, my dad looked at me and said, "Alright son, you ready to go to Auntie's house for the night?" I want to stay with my new baby sister. I nod my head yes anyway and I give my momma a kiss.

"Love you Momma and love you Ana," I say as I grab my dad's hand with one hand while clutching my Gameboy in the other.

It's dark outside and I wish that everyone could just come home now, but my parents say that Ana was born too early and she has to stay there with Momma for a little bit longer. My dad starts up the car and we're on our way. I switch on my Gameboy and try to play Pokémon Yellow in the gaps between the darkness and the street lights illuminated the screen. One second, I'm running around with Pikachu and the next my Gameboy has left my hands. My hair is standing up like I just rubbed my feet on the carpet and touched a balloon, but instead of standing straight up, it feels like it's being yanked from my head and back down into my eyes over and over again. Just like the roller coaster at Six Flags, I'm just tall enough to go on, but threw up my guts afterwards. My seatbelt is digging into my neck so hard it feels like a knife. There are shards of glass everywhere like when Dad and I played baseball inside and I accidentally hit Momma's favorite dishes and shattered them across our apartment. I look around to see my dad and a massive shard of glass piercing his neck. He's staring at me with bloodshot eyes. I sit in silence and stare back at him while blood pools into his mouth and out of his nose and he chokes out one word, "Jameson".

Mom, Ana and I sit at our kitchen table that doubles as a countertop. It's the last day of 8th grade for me. Tomorrow I'll be a high schooler. Mom is making me eggs and bacon, a luxury in our house. Usually, we have generic cereal and milk that's been watered down with so much water that you would think you may as well just throw your cereal under the kitchen sink.

I sit patiently waiting for the food before going off to wait for the bus and see my friends. There are stacks and stacks of white envelopes pushed up against the wall. I know Ana is younger and doesn't think anything of it, but I know they're overdue bills. Ever since dad's accident we've been struggling, but Mom doesn't think either of us notices.

"Are you excited for your last day of school, Jay?" Mom says while she flipped over the bacon to make it extra crispy for me.

"I guess so, I'm really just excited for summer. Maybe I could get a small part-time job?" I say to mom while I eye the white envelopes on the table.

"You know you're too young, baby, but you can definitely try. Start putting your money away for college." She says. I just roll my eyes to myself because I know I will never be able to afford college and so far nothing about it interests me, anyway. I think back to when my dad would play catch with me in the front yard with my special Nerf football. I know I was little, but I always wanted to be a football star. Daydreaming of my dad coming to all of my games, being so proud of me for playing Panther football. Texas loves its football and so did my dad. I remember my mom telling me that when I was being born, my dad couldn't keep his eyes off the Cowboy game while in the delivery room.

After the accident I was talking to plenty of therapists that specialized in PTSD. I just didn't have any drive for anything. I don't care much for anything. I only worry about my mom. She's trying her best.

The lights start to flicker in the apartment, nothing new. Ana continues drawing with pencil on a blank piece of paper. She won't ever let me see until it's finished.

"Ana, how do you want–" Mom starts to say and then drops the whole pan of bacon onto the floor with a crash. I stand up out of my chair and say "Mom, are you okay?" Mom turns around to me. Her eyes are just as bloodshot as my dad's were the night of the accident. She looks at me and tilts her head to the left. She takes the knife off the counter and slits her own throat. Blood starts pooling out of her neck and mouth. Ana sits there like nothing is wrong and continues to draw, humming quietly to herself. I stare at my mom, horrified, and she chokes out the same word the same way my dad did, "Jameson."

I blink once and I'm back to sitting down with my mom turned towards the stove.

"Ana, how do you want your eggs? Ana, stop drawing and answer me, you brat!" Mom says jokingly to her daughter.

"Sorry mom, over-easy is great!" Ana says as I stand up and head straight for my mom, grab her shoulder and yank her toward me. She's completely fine and annoyed that I'm interrupting her cooking.

"Jameson, what is your deal? I'm trying to cook you breakfast! Go set the table and get yourself and your sister some milk," she says to me while cracking an egg on the counter. I step back and rub my eyes. What the hell was that? Maybe I should just chalk it up to puberty or my PTSD that the therapists said I never had.

"Ya mom, sorry," I say as I give her a kiss on the cheek and open the fridge to grab the watered-down milk.

The bell rings. I snap out of my daze and remember I'm at school. The board says Welcome to French II. I grab my bag as we all in unison say au revoir to our teacher and head out to the hallway. This is the most boring part of my day at Odessa High, especially because it's the last class and I'm always looking forward to band practice. I hop in my $750 Pontiac that I saved up to buy since Mom won't let me help with any of the bills. I head to Shawn's house to work on our demo. Shawn lives just a few blocks from me, where the neighborhood starts catering to richer people. Shawn's parents are wealthy and they let him do whatever he wants. His other brother plays Division 1 basketball in Texas so they already have a star athlete in the family. Shawn, on the other hand, is more like me, a nerd that geeks out on all the guitar equipment his parents buy him for his birthday and Christmas, or any time he sneaks their credit card. He also couldn't care less about school. Obviously, I never grew up like that. I'm what you call a "gifted" child. Teachers were always trying to talk Mom into sending me somewhere else besides public school, but we could never afford it. I still try to get straight As to make Mom happy and proud. After Dad's accident, we never got a settlement. It was just an accident, as they called it, and we could never afford to pay someone to stand up for us. I know my mom wants more for me than to just be in a band, but it's all I can ever think about. We have the look, we have the music and I know plenty of bands that have made it through, got signed, and started recording their debut album even before they graduated high school.

I pull up to Shawn's house, my brakes moaning in horror at my abrupt stop and the tire hitting the curb. Shawn's parents are away, staying the weekend at a fancy hotel in southern Texas so they could watch Devon, Shawn's other brother, play. I head through the back gate to Shawn's home studio that was a tiny tool shed in the backyard.

His parents probably paid a fortune to help him soundproof this little slice of heaven. This shed is my safe place like it has been since Shawn and I met freshman year of high school when he let me borrow one of his first guitars and told me to learn tabs. I had no fucking clue what he was talking about, but he made it happen. We started our first band and played the school pep rally that year. Let me tell you, we were awful, maybe we still are, but we're not giving up. I'm dying for a Coors Banquet. I know Shawn has plenty stashed here, so I pop open the door and yell "Hey dude! Beer me!" To my surprise, the studio is empty. I grab myself a beer anyway, knowing his parents aren't home, and head to the back door of their mansion. The door's open, so I head in and upstairs to Shawn's room.

"Shawn, what're you doing? Stop jerking off, we have work to do." No answer even as I get up to his room. His Xbox is on with the Netflix home screen saying "continue watching?". His room is tidy, bed made and everything. I notice a note on his pillow.

COME FIND ME :)

OR ELSE </3

72 HOURS

"What the fuck is this?" I murmur to myself. All of a sudden, I have a splitting headache, I can barely comprehend where I am anymore. I quickly try and open the door to Shawn's bathroom to grab some Advil. I see Shawn standing hunched over the sink, shirtless, staring at himself in the mirror. "Hey man, what're you doing?" I say with my hand holding my head like it has a stab wound. Shawn just continues to look at himself, saliva running out the side of his lips. He starts to laugh uncontrollably.

"You going to save your sister, Jameson?" Shawn says while laughing.

"What do you mean? Shawn, what the hell is going on?" I say as I have to lean on the toilet to keep from falling over.

"You're so fucking gullible, Jameson. He said you had to come find him, but little do you know your little girlfriend Scarlett lead you right to him," Shawn says between his laughter.

"I have no clue what you're even talking about Shawn, I don't have a girlfriend. I came here to finish our demo," I say while the lights start to flicker. Shawn's eyes turn dark and bloodshot. He reaches down his pants leg to his sock and pulls out a pistol.

"You're his next pawn. He loves this game. YOU'RE FUCKED!" Shawn screams, puts the gun to his head and pulls the trigger.

I jolt awake from the smell of something burning. I rush out of the Wendy's manager's office to find the new kid leaving the nuggets in the fryer for too long.

"Come on Jake, you've been working here a week now. You gotta get this stuff down if you want to stay," I say, annoyed at the fact Jake can't seem to learn the ways of Wendy's right and the fact that I got stuck with the dinner rush again. I never envisioned my life at 20 working a manager shift at Wendy's for $11 bucks an hour while the government can swim in my student loan debt in 4 years. Since Shawn's parents moved the entire family in the middle of our senior year and the band didn't work out, I promised my mom I would give it the old college try...but literally. Wait, my subconscious is pounding at my own skull. That was the weirdest dream I had about Shawn. I know his parents moved him away and he would never carry a gun. What the fuck was he saying about me having a girlfriend? I honestly wish, I've never had my so-called glow up yet and I'm also too busy with everything on my plate right now. The phone rings and I can hear someone on staff yell my name.

"He wants to talk to a manager," A shy line cook says to me. I sigh, roll my eyes and pray for 8 p.m. so I can finally go home.

I roll up to our family apartment. I wish I could move out, but Mom says it's not worth paying for the dorms. She's right, but I would love a little freedom. As I yet again hit the curb with my front tires like a clumsy idiot, I see another car in the driveway. My heart sinks. It's the same exact car that hit Dad and me on the way home from the hospital when I was 5. My therapist told my mom I would never really remember anything from the accident, but I feel like no one realizes how vivid a child's memory can be. The car was a dark blue Nissan Altima with all black rims. I even remember hanging upside down, seeing the small dent in the back passenger side door. I run up to the car and see it has the same exact rims, color, and dent in the back. I run up to the front door and swing it wide open.

"Welcome home, Jameson. We've all waited for you so we're having a late dinner. Come sit down!" Mom says to me. Before I can even question who the hell's car is in our small driveway, I see Ana at our makeshift dining-room table and a boy sitting in my usual seat.

"Jameson, this is Henry, my boyfriend. We've been going out for a few months and I thought it was time for him to meet everyone," Ana says.

"Hey man, how's it going?" Henry says while standing up to shake my hand. I reflexively shake his hand and ask, "Where did you get that car?"

"Oh, do you like it? My dad passed it down to me this year. He wanted an upgrade, and when I got my license, this was my 16th birthday present." Henry answered.

"Isn't that nice! What a great gift!" Mom says while still slaving over the stove. I ignore Henry and go straight to Mom and whisper in her ear, "We need to talk."

Mom says out loud, "Can't it wait Jameson? We have company over. Be polite." I sigh and go back to the table.

"You're in my seat." I say to Henry.

"Oh my gosh!" Henry says "I'm so sorry I'll just move over."

"Jay, be nice," Ana says through gritted teeth.

I sit down in my spot as Mom brings over a steaming serving plate of spaghetti and garlic bread. We get through the meal with pleasantries, Mom asking Henry where he's from, where he wants to go to school when he graduates, what he wants to be when he's older, blah blah blah. I stay quiet the whole meal and listen to every single detail Henry spits out.

"So, what's up with your dad?" I say out of nowhere, interrupting the previous conversation.

"Uh, I don't really know what you mean, but he's an ambulance driver for the district," Henry says.

"Does he know that he killed my dad while I was in the backseat of the car?" I say, twirling my noodles onto my fork.

"JAMESON! What has gotten into you?" Mom yells at me.

"I really don't know what you mean, but thank you so much for the meal, Mrs. Hart. I think I better go," Henry says.

"Yeah, run away just like your dad did," I stand up and say it while pointing at the door. Ana walks Henry to his car while she profusely apologizes about my behavior. Mom goes to the sink and starts washing dishes. "Mom I swear to you that's the exact car I saw at the accident that hit us. It even has the same dent and everything." I say.

"Jameson, you were 5 years old, you have no idea what you saw. So just stop with all of this. Your dad's not coming back. There's no reason to bring it up again, it was over a decade ago!" Mom snaps while dropping the plate in the sink, suds splashing out on the counter.

Ana comes back in and says, "Thanks a lot, Jay. I know Shawn moved and your music dreams didn't turn out. You hate your job and college, but that's not MY FAULT," Ana says to me. "I really like Henry and I wanted him to meet my nice older brother whom I look up to, but no, you had to be like this." Ana starts to cry.

"I'm sorry," I say, my words feeling small and meaningless. Ana starts helping Mom clear the table. I know I'm not wanted downstairs at the moment, or it's just my self-pity and self-sabotage ironing the wrinkles of my brain, but either way I start to do the walk of shame up to my room before starting another day of college in the morning.

"I'm going to miss you so much, Jameson." Mom says with tears in her eyes.

"I know Mom. I'm going to miss you both too," I say as I reach for my mom and pull her in for one last hug.

"I hope that crappy car will make it all the way to Denver for you," Ana says with a smile on her face.

"Shut up you little shit head. I will miss you and all your wit, little sis," as I pull her in too for one last group hug. I open the door to my obviously shitty Pontiac, where all my belongings are piled up to the top of the roof in my backseat, and get into the driver's seat. I roll the window down and give one last little wave to the only two people that have had my back my entire life. A single tear rolls down my cheek and I turn right on Main St. I start to buck up as the excitement of moving to Denver and starting a band with this Parker person I met online is now a reality. It seems like Parker wants this as much as me. The US-287 exit comes up to my right as I speed up to hit the interstate. I've always been a nervous driver and I think you can imagine why.

As soon as I get 20 miles past my hometown, I start to calm my nerves and play some of the demos Parker and I have been working on. A semi-truck comes up in the left lane and as soon as I start to pass it, I see for a split second a dark blue Nissan Altima speeding straight toward me before it hits my car. The seatbelt digs into my neck and I can't breathe. The car's engine is so mangled I can hear the metal bend and crack. Everything is in slow motion as the car starts to bounce off with a deafening crunching sound and rolls over the navy blue Altima, me spinning in the air just like when I was a kid. Glass is shattering and almost piercing my eyes. The car stereo is still playing my demos I may never get to finish. My Pontiac flips 8 times before it halts to a stop upside down. I can feel my hair being pulled towards the roof by gravity. I can see out the shattered driver's side window the navy blue Altima pointed towards me with no sign of damage. It revs its engine once, twice, and then the third time, they take their foot off the break. Going as fast as they can straight towards me, everything goes black.

Chapter 8

For a split second I assume I'm dead, but instead I hear a click of a lock come undone and a tiny metal object hitting the floor. As I open my eyes, I can hear footsteps running towards me and feel a warm body embrace me.

"Oh my God, don't ever fucking do that to me again!" yelled Hayden as her tears run down my neck.

"It worked?" I mumble and laugh at the same time before recalling the sound I had heard. "I think something fell to the floor."

Hayden lets me go and we both see the tiny box hanging open under the hand guns. We turn on our flashlights and spot on the chipped wooden floor a single silver key. I reach down and picked it up.

"This has to be the key to the door; we have to go downstairs." I say to Hayden. She nods, our adrenaline spiking more than it had since the twisted game began. We walk to the door, passing the giant statue on the way. I swallow my spit with a cartoonish gulping sound. The key fits perfectly, and the lock falls to the ground. I put Jameson's favorite watch in my pocket. I have a feeling he's fine and it'll be back on his wrist shortly, but I've never been the lucky one.

The door swung inwards to a flight of stairs.

"Obviously, this is the house in the pictures. We already know of a couple rooms down here." Hayden says.

"We try to find Jameson first, okay? If we see anyone else down here, we try and help them, but we need to get Jameson and get the fuck out of here first." I say to Hayden. Deep down I want to save everyone. Lead them out of this godforsaken grave. "I'll go first, please stay close." I say to Hayden as the last thing I see before climbing down the steps is the red record light on her chest.

The creaky stairs immediately ruined any chance of descending unheard, but no one popped out when we reached the bottom. Just like in the pictures, the first door to our left was a perfect lab. It wasn't a regular downstairs bedroom. There was a window on the hallway side, the door, and then two more windows stretching down the hallway to showcase the beautiful stainless-steel lab.

"This is immaculate," Hayden whispers. We cup our hands around our eyes and look through the windows. We could see what looked like a stretcher with IVs attached to a long pole. There were scalpels, staplers, and more surgical tools spread about tables, even saws. I reach for the door, assuming the worst, and sure enough, it's locked. I moved to the next window to see three syringes with the gray liquid inside them laying out on a table. On each there were initials. One of them PJ, the next HP, and the next is turned just enough that I can't make it out.

"Hayden, those have our initials on them, Parker Johnson and Hayden Penny." I whispered.

"I think he's waiting for us, Parker, we shouldn't be down here." Hayden says to me.

"We have to find Jay," I say. "If these are in picture order, this next one is the red room with the girl dead on the wooden chair. We have to keep looking, babe," I say to Hayden as she looks longingly back at the door at the top of the stairs.

"Okay, Parker. Open the door slowly," she says.

The stench hits me just as badly as the one the mystery box emitted. Paper plates and food trays with random slop and scraps were everywhere. If I was locked in here, even without being cut open, it would be miserable. Still in the corner was the stained mattress with no pillow or blankets. The walls were still painted red, but they're marred by brown stains and spatters littering them from floor to ceiling. The chair is still in the middle of the room, too, but there is no one to be found.

"Parker, someone's watching us," Hayden whispers. My eyes follow her pointed finger to the left-hand corner of the room and see a small camera with its red record light blinking.

"I didn't see any monitors anywhere; it must be connected to a phone or an iPad or something like that. It just means there's no more time for exploring and we have to go find Jameson. I can't stand the smell of rotting food, anyways," I say.

Hayden agrees, and we walk back out to the bare hallway. I think the next room is the one where the man was being hanged in the pictures. I shove the door open, a little too impatiently and none too quietly. It's clean inside, and the walls are painted a nice baby blue. Right as I step over the threshold and see the whole room, I reflexively cover my mouth and reach my arm back to keep Hayden from storming in after me.

It's the man that was on our street last night. His leg is in a giant cast and he has butterfly stitches on the top of his head. There was a small TV from the early 2000s with bunny ears attached sitting on the concrete floor. It was playing SpongeBob SquarePants. The man had a giant bowl of what I could tell was cereal. His unbroken leg was chained to the wall, but he didn't seem to mind. He paid no attention to me and continued watching his cartoon, shoving spoonful after spoonful of cereal into his mouth, not caring about spilling milk on his shirt or the floor. SpongeBob had him laughing like he had me when I was a kid. A true knee-slapper. He sits in a folding chair staring at the TV, and he has to have heard me, but he doesn't seem bothered and he wouldn't even look around to see me. I start creeping back out of the room, pushing Hayden back too, and begin to shut the door slowly and quietly as possible without taking my eyes off the man. Before I can get the door shut, he shuts off the TV, gently puts down the empty bowl of cereal and stares in my direction. I watch his dead brown eyes follow me out.

Once I have the door shut, I say, "That's the guy that was in our street, and it's the same guy that handed me the mystery box in our office. We have to hurry. He was chained to the wall, but he saw me," I say, while my hands start to shake and my heart rate spikes.

"Okay baby, calm down, that was the last room in the pictures. It looks like this hallway leads to another living room type thing." Hayden says, taking my hand and leading the way with her flashlight.

We walk into an unfinished part of the basement, and it's so dark we can just make out the wooden bones of the house with pink insulation peeking through, but not much else. Hayden scours the room with her flashlight.

"Jameson!" She gasps and runs toward the corner where Jameson is sitting in a small wooden chair, his hands and feet tied. Clearly unconscious at best, his head is hanging so far back it's almost touching the back of the chair. White foam is drying on the corner of his mouth. I run after Hayden and try to shake Jameson awake.

"Hey buddy, it's us. Wake up, we have to get out of here," I whisper as kindly as possible so I don't freak him out. Jameson starts to wake up in stages, just like I did after surgery. He's groggy, trying to lift his bound hands to rub his eyes.

"Is that really you, Parker?" Jameson says, trying to look around at his surroundings.

"Yeah, man, it's me. Let's get you up and get going, okay?" I say trying to stay calm as I reach for my multitool to try and cut off his bindings.

"What happened to me? You will never fucking guess what I just dreamt. It was like my life flashing before my eyes, but at the same time, some messed up stuff happened."

"I think you might have been injected with something in the shed," I say, "but dude, we can talk about this later, we need to go now." As soon as I get done cutting the last tendril of rope from Jameson's hands, I hear a voice and footsteps on the stairs.

"Jameson, baby, are you okay?" yells Scarlett, "Where are you?"

"Over here babe, I think I'm okay!" Jameson yells as the rope tied around his arms and feet finally severs loose.

"What the fuck are you doing, Jameson? Shut up! We have no idea where she's been." Hayden hisses.

Scarlett finds us and gives Jameson a huge hug. Hayden and I step back, having no idea what to do.

"Where have you been all this time?" I say to Scarlett. She ignores me and just stares at Jameson.

"Hey babe, can you go make me a sandwich?" Scarlett says to Jameson. For a split second I think Scarlett is having a stroke.

"What? Sorry, but no, we have to get out of here. We have to leave now! Are you okay?" Jameson says, trying to look Scarlett closer in her eyes.

Scarlett sighs, "Well, that sucks. I thought you would be another one. I had fun while it lasted, but we have no use for you anymore. You definitely were one of the cutest ones."

"What're you talking about?" Jameson spits out. Before any of us have the chance to react, Scarlett takes out a knife and plunges it through the side of Jameson's neck. One foul swoop in and out as blood starts pouring to the floor. Jameson's hands rocket up to his neck trying to keep the blood inside as his legs fail him. Jameson hits the floor gurgling wet blood out of his mouth as he tries to say words no one would be able to understand.

"Jay!" I scream and before I know it everything is black.

"I have no fucking clue what you're talking about!" Hayden yells and wakes me up out of my slumber. I'm back upstairs next to Hayden, hands and feet tied like Jameson's were. Jay, I think to myself. I just lost my best friend. Never in my life did I think it would end up like this. We were supposed to be heroes. I come out of my daze and notice I have a pounding, splitting headache. We're back upstairs sitting on the pews. Scarlett is in front of the giant statue with a man. He had to be at least in his late forties, salt and pepper hair with a nice beard connecting all the way up his sideburns. The top of his head was somewhat balding. The man was thin besides a beer belly and he's wearing a cream-colored sweater and jeans.

"Welcome back, Parker! Sorry about your head, I hit you a little too hard with this trusty old pan!" the man says. "I was just asking your girlfriend about her old job and her old boss."

"Please let us go, we came here and found you, my friend is gone, can we please just go home?" I start to plead.

"Hasn't anyone told you begging is unattractive?" the man says.

"Let us out of here!" Hayden screams. All of a sudden, Scarlett slaps Hayden across the face.

"Now Scarlett, please be a little more gentle with our guests. You never know how the serum will affect them," the man says.

"Sorry, dad, but I've been waiting days to do that!" Scarlett says with a satisfied smile.

Dad? I think to myself, realizing finally that this has been a set-up all along.

"Since I know all about you two, let me introduce myself," The man says with a polite smile.

"My name is Ed Whitmore, earth leader for Azazela, and this, as you know, is my daughter Scarlett, also an earth leader for the great Azazela."

"I believe I've been put on this earth to give, well, earth and all its people to her, Azazela. She has worked too hard for too many years, but I think I've found the solution for her, and I think I can perfect it with your help, Hayden," he says, as though we had been working alongside him to find it all this time. Before we could process this or give him an answer, he continued.

"God doesn't have a chance. I've been watching you two ever since you landed yourself a job at Ender Industries before the pandemic. You and your boss, Greg, seemed to be getting along very, very well! I actually thought I lost track of you two once the world went up in flames with the pandemic. I honestly thought I failed, and Azazela was here to pin a plague on humanity. I bet she's tired of waiting for me. Anyway, my boy downstairs loves those YouTube channels, and one day he was watching yours. I recognized that pretty face of yours, Hayden, and was surprised to see the ambitious Parker by your side. The biggest theme on YouTube was the dark web mystery box and all it took was one email to Parker to get you guys to catch the bait. So, let's talk about Greg shall we Hayden?"

I look at Hayden and whisper, "Do you know what he's talking about?"

Hayden ignores me, and Ed Whitmore goes on, "I know what you two were making, I was a part of the team. You don't remember me, because I was the one putting the AI robots together. Constructing their limbs and making sure they could walk. I was never one for programming, but you guys didn't exactly program the robots, did you? You created a serum to inject into the robots to make them more human-like. Little did you know, Greg was committing tax fraud and the company went under. They blamed the pandemic for the loss of your job and mine, too, and things seemed hopeless for me, until Azazela came to me. She told me I was on the right path, but I had to figure it out myself. Once no one was around, just before we were shut down for good, I stole vials of your special liquid and brought it to my own lab, for human trials."

"That's impossible, you can't just inject humans with that stuff. It was for machines only. There're so many elements in that serum that cannot go into a living body!" Hayden says.

"Oh, but you're wrong! I've injected countless humans, I'm pretty sure you've seen some of their remains in my fridge. I'm not a monster, those are just keepsakes. I think you've also met my boy a couple of times. He's downstairs now as we speak, and he paid you a visit last night. He's the only one so far whose mental functions largely remain the same as before the injection, but he's now 100 percent obedient to me," Whitmore says. "Speaking of the keepsakes, well–."

Scarlett speaks up, cutting him off. "Cut off their ear so when you say a command, it can't go in one ear and out the other. Cut off the toe so they won't be able to stand on their own two feet. Even after death, Azazela can find ways to control, but we're doing our best to make it easier."

"You guys are insane, none of this is possible. What are you even talking about?" My voice rises and I'm shouting by the end.

"You have no idea how long I've waited for this, Parker. You lost your friend? Tough luck. I've lost everything, but it'll be worth it. We'll be standing by her side when everything comes to fruition." All vestiges of civility disappear from his mannerisms and he's screaming and pounding the front pews with his hands, punctuating his speech. "Hayden, I know Greg had a secret ingredient, and I need it now!"

"My relationship with Greg was never what you think it was," Hayden chokes out. "Yes, I was the lead on the robots, but Greg didn't tell me any secrets or anything like that. He kept trying to get me alone because...because–" Hayden starts crying and can barely say the next words. "He told me a pretty girl like me can't be gay and I need to sleep with a real man to get my mind off my 'girlfriend'."

That word, "girlfriend" was like a shot to my heart. I hated being called feminine terms. I could understand why Hayden never told me this about her boss. She always seemed so happy at that job before the pandemic took it away from her.

"I swear Greg was nothing more than disgusting to me and he never let me in on anything secret. I can't help you!" Hayden yelled.

"STOP LYING TO ME!" Whitmore booms. "If you won't tell me, then I guess we have no other choice, pretty girl. You'll either tell me, or I'll just kill you like your little friend. Scarlett, do it," he says.

"No, stop stop stop!" I scream, frantically trying to figure out what I can do next to save the love of my life.

"Please, Hayden, if you know anything, please tell them! Please!" I say, tears again falling from my eyes. I'm not even able to wipe them off because my hands are tied behind my back. Then I remember the multitool. I had put it in my back pocket as soon as Scarlet showed up and hugged Jameson downstairs. I begin trying to maneuver my bound hands to my pocket without drawing attention to myself.

"Don't you touch me, bitch!" Hayden yells and spits at Scarlett, who's walking toward her with the syringe in hand.

"This'll be fun," laughs Scarlett. My eyes lock onto Hayden and I whisper "I love you" as the needle disappears into her neck. I manage to reach the multitool and pry a few random attachments on their hinges at once, miraculously including the serrated knife, and start sawing away at the rope as quickly and quietly as I can. I need to save her, she's all I have left.

Chapter 9

Hayden

I walk off the bus to the picture-perfect house I've lived in my whole life. The front yard a perfect shade of freshly cut green, concrete steps 1, 2, 3, and 4 marking the path up to the beautiful oak front door. Flowers planted on both sides of the stairs. Mostly pansies and roses, Mom's favorite. On my tenth birthday a couple months ago, she let me plant some bleeding hearts near her perfect roses. I think that memory of my mom and I planting my favorite flower together will be branded on my brain for the rest of my life. Birds are chirping and butterflies are flying all around the garden. Monarch butterflies flying as high as the point where the white siding meets the dark blue tiles of the roof. This is a dream home, as my dad used to call it. I've never wished for a move a day in my life, and I always get to climb the trees in the backyard with the squirrels. Dad was always really handy. I have a perfect wooden tree house in the backyard with a tire swing hanging below. Getting all four seasons in small-town Colorado, I couldn't even pick my favorite. Smiling brightly after a great day of elementary school, I walk those concrete stairs up to the front door and pull it open.

I always look forward to my mom's big hugs and greetings, but she's nowhere to be seen. I think to myself that she's probably making an extra amazing after-school snack for me and lost track of the time. I head to the kitchen, where everything is packed up and tidy Usually my mom is home making snacks and taking care of the house while my dad works. I love my mom being home for me. The other kids talk about how fun after-school care is, but I'm perfectly fine coming home to my mom. I look out the back window to see if she's out in the yard taking care of things. I see my dad's car in the makeshift driveway. He never uses that driveway unless he's in a hurry to get in the house because he forgot something to bring to work. I start yelling, "Mom?" up and down the house until I reach the stairs to go up to the bedrooms. I open the door and peak into my parents' room.

The first thing I see is my mom curled up in a fetal position crying while my dad is rubbing her back. She's gently sobbing and my heart sinks. My dad finally sees me and gets up to take me to the other room.

"Do you think you can make yourself your own snack today?" my dad says. I ignore the question and ask, "What's wrong with Mom, what happened?"

"Well, Hayden, God decided that the baby wasn't ready for this world and took him back. Mommy is just really upset about it, but she will get better. Please try and be a big girl and put on a brave face for Mom, okay?"

A few months later, we still decide to celebrate the due date for my unborn baby brother. My mom hasn't been the same since that day after school. I figured out with the help of our slow family computer with an ethernet cable that my mom had a miscarriage. The baby couldn't live in my mom's belly like I could. The due date celebration was supposed to be fun, but it honestly just made everyone sad. My new nanny, Marie, baked a cake for the occasion. I liked Marie. She was younger than my parents and loved to play with me all the time, whatever game I wanted to play. She was the one making me after-school snacks now that Mom cries in her room most days. Marie told me my mom would get better soon and I hoped and prayed to God that she was right.

That night, after Marie tucks me into bed, I hear a whisper:

"Hayden, come out to the tree house to play."

"Who's there?" I whisper back, starting to panic.

"Just come on, it'll be fun!"

The door to my room creaks open, but there's no one there. I start walking down the stairs with my Mickey Mouse blankie and open the back door to the huge backyard. There's a tiny chill in the air so I grab my coat and look out beyond the trees. In the tree house I see a small light, almost moving. I realize it's lit by candlelight and start heading over. I think to myself that nothing can hurt me, I'm in my own backyard with my own tree house. Usually, the tire swing is slowly moving back and forth, but I don't see it hanging anymore. I gently walk up the latter and boost myself up on the wooden platform. In the tree house there is a boy, about 5 years old.

He looks at me and says, "Alright, here's some chalk. Let's play tic-tac-toe on the ceiling!"

"Who are you? Shouldn't you be home?" I say to the boy.

"What to do you mean, Hayden? This is my home. I'm your brother, don't you remember?

"You're being silly!" The boy says to me.

"No, you're not. Dad said he had to go back with God," I say, confused.

"Hayden, today is my birthday. I thought you would draw me a cake in chalk and wish me a happy birthday like we always do. You must've been dreaming about what Dad said to you," the boy says in a discouraged tone.

"I guess so, but I think I should go wake up Marie and have her come help us," I say.

"Who's Marie?" the boy says.

"You know Marie, the nanny that has to take care of us now that Mom..." I trail off.

"Mom is fine!" The boy giggles. "We just had her amazing chocolate cake! You're being so weird, Hayden! Now wish me a happy birthday!"

"Okay, okay! I'm sorry, I guess I'm just really sleepy!"

I smile at the boy and start drawing a birthday cake on the ceiling of the tree house. Once I'm done, the boy says "That's the best one you've drawn yet! Now sing!" I laugh and give him the eraser so that when I'm done singing, he can "blow" out the candles. I start singing:

Happy birthday to you,

Happy birthday to you,

Happy birthday dear...

"Wait, what's your name?" I say to the boy.

The boy smiles and reaches behind him. His small hands grab the rope that was attached to the tire swing. The rope is already tied into a noose.

"My name's Parker and you're going to watch me die!" The boy shouts just before throwing the noose around his neck and jumping out of the tree house door. I hear the bones in his neck snap while the tree branches creak to keep the house stable. I scramble over to the window and see his little body swinging back and forth out of my view. I scream.

"Hayden, snap out of it and write your crush on the wall with this blue chalk," a teenage girl says to me.

I look at Taylor and grab the blue chalk out of her hand. I see dozens of boys' names written on the ceiling of the tree house. Most are crossed out.

"I know you have a big crush on Zach. Just write his name, it's pretty obvious," Taylor says to me, laughing.

"Sorry, I guess I just spaced out for a minute," I say as I start to write ZACH next to the crossed-out STEVE I put up a couple months ago.

"You know he'll never go out with me? He didn't even dance with me at freshman Monogram even though we were literally pushed together," I say to Taylor.

"Yeah, but this year's different! We're sophomores and he's finally going to see you!" Taylor assures me.

"Maybe you're right, I just don't know." I say.

I never really had great self-esteem, even though my dirty blonde hair attracted all the boys I didn't want. I've dated here and there, even had this boy that would give me the entire world, but I have no idea why I couldn't love him. I never really felt that initial spark besides a teenage lust.

As the night went on, after Marie helped us make some dinner, we lay in my queen-size bed and played on our Motorola EnVs.

"I thought Ashley was supposed to sleep over, too?" Taylor asked.

"Now that I think of it, me too. You should shoot her a text." I say.

Taylor starts typing on her horizontal keyboard and soon after her phone buzzes.

"She just texted me back and said 'are you with Hayden? I need to tell her something but I think it needs to go through you first'," Taylor read the text out loud.

"That's weird, text her back and tell her to tell you!" I say as anxiety fills my stomach all the way to my fingertips. Taylor nods and texts her back at lightning speed.

"Holy shit," Taylor says.

"What the hell, tell me!" I say as I grab the phone out of her hands.

Ashley: Well to be completely honest with you guys I've been really struggling with my sexuality, I think I'm Bi and I think I really like Hayden. I'm really nervous to tell you guys and that's why I didn't come over tonight. I know it's weird and we are all best friends, but I can't keep it in anymore.

"Wow, I don't know what to say. I mean, I'm not gay," I say to Taylor.

"I mean we obviously can't hold it against her, you know? It might be weird for a little while, but you should text her back. Just tell her it's you." Taylor says to me. Still having Taylor's phone in my hand, I start to type back.

Taylor: Hey this is Hayden. I'm really happy that you told me and I still want to be friends with you, do you think we can hang out this weekend and talk about it?

Ashley: I don't really want to talk about it anymore, but I would love to hang out with you. We can just hang out and watch music videos like we normally do.

Taylor: Of course! You sure you don't want to come over tonight?

Ashley: No that's okay. I'll see you this weekend.

I hand the phone back to Taylor and we both just start laughing and rolling around my queen-sized bed out of pure shock of what just happened.

"Didn't she just write Gabe on the treehouse crush ceiling a couple days ago?" Taylor says.

"Yeah, but she was probably just playing it off, you know?" I say. "You're probably right. Whatever. Put in *Juno* already and let's look at pictures of emo boys!" Taylor says.

I get up and go to the DVD player put in the disk and press play. We spend the rest of the night looking on the computer and watching *Juno* over and over again. My mind's in a different place. I cannot stop thinking about Ashley and why she even likes me. Thinking about the text message over and over again and trying and failing to keep the butterflies away from my stomach.

The last week of summer always flies by, but I know tonight I get to hang out with Ashley. I don't know why I'm so excited, nothing is going to happen. It's just going to be us girls watching music videos and eating snacks.

"Hey Marie, I'm headed over to Ashley's tonight so I won't be home for dinner," I say.

"That sounds good to me, but maybe you should go ask your mom. She's up and doing good today," Marie says.

My stomach dropped. It's always good to hear that Mom is awake and being just a tiny bit normal. It's been five years since her miscarriage and the doctors diagnosing her with manic depressive disorder. They've tried every pill in the book, but it always seems like she's on suicide watch. My dad works so much, but he's always here for me if needed. Plus, I have Marie.

She's been the older sister I've always wanted. Even on Mom's good days, she always goes back to the bad.

"I do feel neglected sometimes," as I would tell my therapist, but I always feel selfish. I love my mom. The first ten years of my childhood were perfect. Maybe I should be giving her more slack.

I head up the red carpeted stairs to her bedroom, usually where she sits and watches game shows.

"Hey Mom, how's it going today? I think I'm going to head over to Ashley's if that's okay," I say to my mom, who's up and cleaning off her side table.

"Hey baby! Yes, that's totally fine, even though I'm going to cook your favorite pork sandwiches tonight. You can have some tomorrow though, I'll cook a bunch!" She says to me.

"You're going to cook?" I say, very confused, because my mom hasn't been in the kitchen besides grabbing herself chocolates when Marie is busy taking care of me for years.

"Yes hon, I feel really great. I had a visitor last night," she says to me.

"Mom, no one was here last night besides Taylor," I say.

"No, baby, this angel named Azazela came to me and said your brother is with her and everything is going to be okay," my mom replies.

"What are you talking about?" I say to her.

"I have a lot to do, baby. Go get ready and head to Ashley's. I'll see you tomorrow. I love you!" She says as she kisses me on the cheek and rushes downstairs.

I'm stunned. Hopefully Marie can take care of this, and I bet she will be back in bed by tonight and won't come out till Christmas. There's me again, though, being selfish and negative.

I hop in my 1999 red slug bug and head over to Ashley's house. I got very lucky having my birthday in August so I could get my license last year. I walk into her house without knocking and head downstairs to the basement where her room resides. No one is home as per usual. She doesn't get along with her stepmother very well so they might be out and about and Ashley refused to go.

"Hey, what's up?" Ashley says as I get down to her room. She won't look me in the eye.

"Hey, you know this doesn't have to be awkward, you know?" I say to her with a big smile.

"You're right, I'm sorry. Let's just pretend I didn't even say anything. I have snacks and some new vinyls we can listen to," Ashley says.

"Sweet!" I say as I jump on the bed right next to her.

Our arms barely touch, but I can feel the electricity flowing between us. I have butterflies in my stomach going all the way to my toes, making them curl in every which way, and I have no idea why. Ashley gets up and puts a new vinyl on her record player. We start eating chips and snacks and talk about everything, just like normal. Hours go by as we start looking at boys on the internet and laughing at dumb jokes.

"So, I think I'm going to try and go out with Gabe," Ashley says to me. "I think that I'm ready. I'm going to sleep with him."

"No way!" I say, giggling. "I've barely even made out with a boy; I don't even know if I'm doing it right. All the boys that like me I just can't imagine even touching them. I just want to date Donnie Darko."

Ashley laughs and says, "Hayden, everyone wants to date Donnie Darko! But I mean, I can help with that."

"Help with what?" I say as I shove another Oreo into my mouth.

"Learning how to kiss and stuff like that," Ashley mumbles.

For some reason, my heart bursts with joy and I can feel the butterflies everywhere in my body.

"I mean, I don't know, do you really want to?" I say to Ashley in an embarrassed tone.

She places her hand on my face, her thumb running over my bottom lip. Ashley then kisses me. I pull back in utter surprise, but then I look into her green eyes and go back in. Our lips move together like a ballerina dancing. Hands in hair and lust in our guts. She takes off my shirt and I'm all in. This is the feeling I've been searching for, so uncharted so hot. She's beautiful and pure, but at the same time so sinful.

The button on my pants pops off with her fingertips. Halfway there to paradise. Suddenly, in the corner of her bedroom, the closet door rips open, shredding Ashley's posters off the wall. The room becomes dark. The light shining from the closet as My mom and dad march through the closet, pointing at me.

"Hayden, what the hell are you doing? Don't ever come back to the house. You're a disgrace. A disgusting disgrace to this family and God!" My mom yells. She starts bawling into my dad's arms as I reach for my T shirt. Taylor bursts through the door next.

"You're gay? I can't believe it. After all the times you told us you weren't. You're just a liar. How can I be friends with a liar?" Taylor says to me and rolls her eyes and goes and sits by the record player.

"What the fuck is happening?" I turn to Ashley and say.

Ashley looks at me and smiles, "You're just a fucking dyke, aren't you? Everyone knew, but you," Ashley starts to laugh and is joined in by my dad, mom and Taylor.

All of them laughing hysterically, they all start chanting, "Dyke, dyke, dyke, dyke."

"Go back in the closet fag!" Ashley screams at me over the chanting. I don't know what else to do, so I start walking into the closet as they continue to chant. I go back into the closet just to see the little boy hanging by the rope of the tire swing looped around his neck. Back and forth he swings in the closet. He opens his eyes, grabs my dirty blonde hair. The closet doors swing shut and everything goes black.

"So, you said you graduated from Montana State University with a bachelor's in business management with honors?" Greg says to me.

I'm in a high-rise building in the middle of downtown Denver. The office I'm in is made up of glass walls and I can see the Rocky Mountains looking West.

"Uh...yes, that's correct. I graduated last year and moved back home. Montana was too cold," I say to Greg as he continued to look through my resume.

"Well, you're in luck. We are in desperate need of a project manager for our new sector of the company, and you look like a perfect fit. Now, this is top secret, and we can't really tell anyone what's going on, alright?" Greg says.

"I'll take whatever you're offering, Mr. Mooden," I say.

"Please, just call me Greg. I'll see you tomorrow bright and early, let's say 8 o'clock for orientation."

"That sounds great. Thank you so much, Greg." I say. Greg stands up with me and opens the door for me to exit. He put his hands on my lower back as I walked out the door. I try my best to ignore it.

Two months into the project, I'm promoted to senior project manager. Ender Industries was going to be the next big thing, I could feel it. I oversee scheduling for the morning and the night shift scientists. We've had to work day and night to get these guys going. The main focus of the project has been to create these AI robots that could be controlled to work as cashiers, servers, nannies, you name it. We're in a race with other tech companies to be the first to release these creatures to the market.

What we have going for us that no one else does was that we didn't put microchips into the robot to create the AI. Greg and his team concocted a liquid, kind of like how blood runs through our veins, but this was going through the robots' human-like ports.

"We're so close, Hayden," Greg says to me at our weekly Monday morning meeting. "We just have to make it so the robots don't have personal opinions. I want them to do what they're told so humankind can have more relaxing lives. Plus, we can make billions!" He says, laughing.

"I agree. The schedule is doing great. People aren't getting burnt out, and we are ahead of our quarterly budget," I say.

"You know we make a great team, don't you, Hayden?" He says as he comes out from behind his desk to sit on the front of it, legs spread. "I pay you very well and I know you work hard, but this could be more, you know?"

"I have a partner already, Greg," I say to him, getting very uncomfortable.

"Oh yeah, your girlfriend. Don't you think you need a real man to satisfy you?" Greg slips his body off the desk and takes my chin in his hands.

I rip my face away and say, "I'm going to get back to work. There's a lot of stuff that needs to be done today."

Greg sighs and says, "I'll see ya later," then takes out his phone to start scrolling aimlessly like nothing had happened.

Tears fill my eyes as I left his office. This wasn't the first time this situation has happened. First it was at a company dinner, and then the parking lot. I had hoped it wouldn't escalate to the actual office, but it has. I need this job; I don't know what else to do. I don't want anyone to see my tears, so I let my head hang and stare at the floor back to the AI room. On my way, I bump shoulders with a man covered in grease with salt-and-pepper hair. He held a detached robot arm in his hand.

"I'm sorry, ma'am. Are you okay?" the man says.

I just nod and wipe my eyes as my heels echo through the rest of the hallway.

Chapter 10

"You sure have made this fun, Parker. I've always been one for theatrics," Whitmore says, laughing. "It's only a matter of time before Hayden wakes and we can see if the serum takes hold."

Scarlett overhears and says, "Please, daddy, can I be the one to ask her the question?"

Whitmore looks at his gorgeous dark-skinned light-eyed daughter and says, "Of course baby. If it takes, you'll be in charge anyway, after all the lab tests. Now, let's wait and pray."

I try and ignore them as best I can as Scarlett and her father sit on the front-most pew and bow their heads into their hands. I look over at Hayden, her head hanging backwards over the pew, a tiny trail of foam dripping from the corner of her mouth. My hands ache in the awkward positions they take as I try to cut the rope around my wrists. This is my chance, as both Scarlett and Whitmore are now sitting with their eyes closed, facing that giant metal statue.

I start to think of every single horror movie I've ever watched. I know I'm not strong enough to fight off both of them. I've never been a fighter. I look around the house for things I could use to defend myself, but instead I only notice yet again how inhabitable this house really is. Does this so-called family live in another house around Denver, or do they each take up a pew and a dirty mattress downstairs and call that living?

The blood-stained carpet underneath the four small wooden pews is making my stomach turn. All I can smell are those body parts that were on my kitchen counter—admittedly, the second we should've called the fucking cops. There might be a way I could sneak around and push the statue right on top of their smug bodies, but I have no idea if that statue would even budge.

I start to wonder how they even got this horrendous statue in this house in the first place. There's fucking nothing in this house besides boarded-up windows, peeling wallpaper and... the door.

My heart once again drops to the pit of my stomach. It must have happened when I was knocked out, because there's no other way.

When we arrived at the murder house, opening the door felt like opening a tiny wooden cabin door. It was on the verge of breaking off the hinges. Looking around now, I notice that the door is enforced with a stainless-steel barrier. Ed Whitmore might be insane, but he's not stupid. There's no escape with them still alive in this house.

Finally, I manage to break my hands free, inertia causing my knife to bump the wooden pew. I hold my breath, but neither Scarlett and Whitmore seemed to notice. I could just barely hear them whispering their prayers to the "Great Azazela." Half was in a language I couldn't understand and half was about making the serum take a hold of their sacrifices, also known as Hayden and me.

I start working on the ties around my feet. I wish I never had that fucking panic attack in Home Depot or else I would've picked out a better, sharper knife. Still glancing around, I finally see my last option--the guns on the wall. Surely if I throw down the levers to the wrong numbers, they'll fire, right? If I push

Hayden down with her arms still bound, the bullets wouldn't penetrate the thick wood of the pew. If I get up and run, I think Scarlett and Whitmore would stand up and the bullets would ricochet and hit everyone, including me.

I don't want to die, but I would rather die for Hayden than get injected with that shit. This is my only option.

I'll wait just until Hayden wakes, and I'll leave the knife behind her. She's such a smart girl. She will have time to figure out how to open the door or get the barricades off the windows with everyone upstairs dead. The boy downstairs is chained up. She will move on from me.

I pray to whatever god there actually is that Hayden will wake up normal, just like Jameson. I see the red lights of both our cameras attached to our chests. They're still recording. Hayden needs to get out of here and show the world what fucked up things are happening in Denver. Police need to be involved and find more of this cult if there are any.

Snapping me out of my planning, I hear Hayden say, "Baby, where are we?"

I look at her, quickly putting my hands back behind the chair, and say, "Please trust me. You need to get those cameras out of here. I'm sorry, baby. I love you so much. You have to do what I say."

"Look who's awake, Daddy!" Scarlett says in a bright tone.

"Welcome back, Hayden! How was the serum? Hopefully delightful!" Whitmore says as he stands up from his kneeling position and waves Scarlett toward us.

Scarlett looks as excited as an elementary school kid getting off the bus to go to the dinosaur museum. She reaches the pew just before ours and kneels on the wooden bench with her arms crossed, right in front of Hayden.

“What’s going on, Parker? My head hurts so bad. I just wanna go home,” Hayden moans quietly.

I gently shush her, wishing I could take all the pain away instead. I wish I could run my hands through her hair and have her lean on my chest while I give her tiny forehead kisses. I wish we could just go back to lying on the couch with Boba, watching the worst TV shows in the history of the world, but it wouldn’t matter because I was safe with them.

My heart is breaking hearing Hayden say those words to me, and I finally really, truly grasp that this is all my fault. I’m not the hero, I’m the villain. I made my best friend and the love of my life come to this house for a show. I’m drowning in self-pity and snap out of it as fast as the realization popped into my head. *Shut the fuck up, Parker, I say to myself.* I *need* to get her out of here.

“Hey Hayden, can you go make me a sandwich?” Scarlett says with a small laugh. I’m holding my breath, and I can tell everyone else in the room is also waiting for Hayden’s answer.

“Yeah Scarlett... you can fucking go to hell!” Hayden screams in her face. My own breath pops out of my mouth in a relieved gasp.

“You ugly good for nothing bitch!” Scarlett screams back and pulls out the same knife she used on Jameson.

“Scarlett, don’t!” Whitmore yells. “You know we need her alive. It’s a damn shame, but I knew it wouldn’t be that easy. She still knows something; I can feel it.”

“She doesn’t know a damn thing, Dad! Whoever this Greg guy was obviously just wanted in her pants. We still have one left to do experiments on! We don’t need her!” Scarlett whines.

"Shut your little whore mouth!" Whitmore yells and yet again bangs his hands on the hard wooden pew for her attention. "Go see if your brother needs anything."

"But Dad, I wanna stay!" Scarlett says.

"Go, now!" Whitmore screams.

"He's not my brother."

Scarlett tries to say it under her breath, but everyone in the room can hear.

I know now's my chance. Whitmore and Scarlett aren't paying attention to either of us anymore. Hayden got them fighting. That's my girl, I think to myself as I look over at her and see that she's still groggy from the injection.

I whisper to Hayden, "Please trust me. I love you so much."

Before she can even ask what I'm talking about, in my head I'm already counting to 1...2...3. Just like I did before leaning in to kiss Hayden for the first time. On three, I shove Hayden as hard as I can with my right arm. With her hands still tied, her balance is off, and she tumbles right back onto the seat of the pew with the wooden back rest blocking anything that would try to penetrate behind her.

I jump up as fast as I could and raced towards the gun trap. I dive and my hands grasp the cold metal of the remaining numbered letters. I close my eyes and realize this is the end for me, but this is also the end of Scarlett and Whitmore. Hayden will be safe. Hayden will get out of here.

Instead of a final bang of bullets and gunpowder, all I hear is a clap clap clap as slow as can be and coming right from Whitmore.

"You got out of the bindings! What a smart little boy you are! You think I would really make a trap that could potentially kill you before we could even try and inject you? Before we even let you meet the great Azazela? Like I said, I love theatrics, but come on!" Whitmore says with a sinister laugh.

"We sure got you there, but this isn't over, Parker, this is just the beginning. Scarlett, if you will?" Scarlett goes and sits right next to Hayden with her knife pointed at her jugular.

"So, Parker, if you'll just come here and sit next to me, Hayden won't be in any trouble, and we can at least just get your feet back in some rope, what do you say?"

I finally overcame the courage to speak up again, "Fuck you. You already said you need her."

"Well, she sure doesn't need her fingers and toes, or maybe even her tongue, if we can get her to write!" Scarlett says with a smile as she slides the dull flat side of the blade all over Hayden's body.

I don't know what else to do. My mind is blank and out of options. There was no secret trap. The key would've fallen out no matter what levers I pulled down. I feel defeated and nauseous as I made my way up to the front of the pews.

"That's a good boy, Parker." Whitmore says.

"I'm not a boy, you fat pig," I spit back at him, and as soon as the words came out of my mouth I feel a fist slam into my gut. All the air leaves my lungs and I'm hunched over under the metal statue.

"You know, this would be a lot easier without all the dirty words and non-cooperation," Whitmore says as he begins tying my feet and hands back together with rope. "Find the object Parker used to cut loose and bring Hayden up here with us. We need to pray together," he says, as he yanks me up by my hair and forces me to kneel in front of the giant statue.

Scarlett brings her father Hayden and the small multitool I tried to hide behind her back. She forces Hayden to kneel, and Whitmore starts.

"Great Azazela I come bearing three sacrifices, one already lost to death, one that worked on our serum we put in my boy and the other, a self-proclaimed hero. Scarlett and I need your guidance. Let us be your vessel. Please, Scarlett, if you will, can you go get the Bufo Alvarius and your choice of blood?" Ed Whitmore says.

Scarlett nods her head, goes into the kitchen, and comes back with what looks like a red mixed cocktail and hands it to her dad.

I know that name from somewhere, Bufo Alvarius. My mind keeps returning back to Jameson for some reason. It's one of those memories where it's on the tip of your tongue and you would rather die than not remember, it's bugging you so damn bad.

Then it hits me.

Jameson and I, monthly, hit up a new brewery that does trivia. If I can tell you anything, we aren't good at all, but we usually try and get drunk enough not to care if anyone notices that we are Googling the answers in the bathroom. We never win, anyways. This core memory came back like a freight train.

The question was "What animal produces not venom, but a poison on their skin that functions as a hallucinogen?" The answer was the Bufo Alvarius frog.

Jameson wanted to find one so bad on the internet, just to get a little high. He had a thing about trying all the designer drugs. I also start thinking about Whitmore saying something about blood. I can't get the thought of human blood out of my head. It was all over the blanket in the mystery box, and for some reason, I no longer think it was fake.

I try to speak up, but right when the first suggestion of the word “monster” comes out of my mouth, Whitmore yells, “I didn’t tell you to speak yet, boy! We’re about to start praying. The ritual is underway.”

I look at Hayden, wanting to whisper my realization in her ear, but I’m distracted by the realization that her body is swaying back and forth and there’s sweat dripping from her forehead.

Scarlett sees me notice Hayden’s poor state and says, “Yeah, we never really know why the human body rejects the serum, but it seems like it acts as a poison. The only one it hasn’t done it to is my ‘brother’ downstairs,” she says, while making air quotes with both her hands.

“What do you mean?” I shoot out before Whitmore can shut me up. “We have to do something; she has to go to the hospital! Please, I’m begging you, she’s not well!”

“Stop! Both of you!” Whitmore yells. His hands have to be stinging from slamming them down on the hard wooden pews so many times. “It’s time. While I’m being the vessel, please hold your knife up to Parker’s neck so they both won’t try and do anything. I also do need something from both of you...repeat after me: cor mentis corpus imperium”.

“I’m not fucking saying a word for you, you freak! What you’re drinking is nothing but a hallucinogen, it won’t do shit for you! It won’t summon anything but from your own fucked up mind!” I yell as Scarlett presses the knife to my neck a tiny bit harder so a trickle of blood pools down to my collarbones.

“Like I said, Parker, I don’t need most of your body to conduct human trials on you. Do it, Scarlett.”

Scarlett takes the knife from my neck and walks over to Hayden.

"Finally," she says under her breath.

She takes the knife and slams it into the side of Hayden's thigh. Hayden screams in pain, but Scarlett grabs her bound wrist and keeps her upright still kneeling on the now bleeding leg.

"Stop! Don't touch her again!" I say as tears start rolling down my eyes. I feel completely helpless.

"Oh, I will stop, Parker, as long as you chant 'cor mentis corpus imperium' over and over again while I drink the blessed blood of Azazela's victims. You too, Hayden, between wincing, as much as you can. I know Scarlett is smart enough not to hit anything major," Whitmore says.

Scarlett winks at her dad and comes back over to me. Knife pushed back into my bleeding neck.

Whitmore looks at me once again and simply says, "Start."

I start chanting the words I cannot understand and so does Hayden, through labored breaths. I have no other option and my anxiety is bubbling up from my legs. I need to get Hayden to a hospital. Maybe just playing by their rules will get us out of here.

Scarlett has moved about a foot away from me, and she's chanting along with us. Whitmore takes the blood-red cup in his hands and drinks it down to the last drop. He falls to his knees, the glass cup rolling away to stop at my feet.

Whitmore starts yelling like he's in excruciating pain and heaving like a dog. I look over at Hayden. Sweat is still dripping down the side of her head, but she's also staring intently on the reaction that Ed Whitmore is having.

Suddenly, Whitmore gets up like nothing happened. He starts staring at the side of the metal statue like someone is there.

"Thank you for answering me, your greatness, I just don't know what else to do. The serum didn't work on Hayden, and I can't get her to tell me anything about the missing ingredient," Whitmore says.

Then, all of a sudden, I hear a woman's voice answering him. The only problem was it came from Ed Whitmore himself, answering his own question. The voice coming out of the older salt and pepper-haired man was angelic, to say the least. It was the most calming coo, like a mother saying goodnight to her child. I stumble over my chant in shock that that voice was coming out of this man.

"Ed, it was never about Hayden. She told the truth; you were just too blind to see it. I never sent you out here for her, it's Parker that holds our will."

I look back over to Hayden and her eyes say it all. We both have no idea what to do. I look at the camera on her chest. The red light, still recording, thank God. I don't think anyone would believe this story if we weren't documenting it.

Ed Whitmore's own voice returns and says, "I'm so sorry Azazela, I know I've disappointed you and I'm sorry I had to come back to you for guidance. Parker is here, he will be next."

The women's voice came back out of him and says, "Parker goes by 'they,' Ed. Even though these people hold the key to our world control, that does not mean we can deny their simplest wishes. You've done the work, but I'm getting tired and bored of your theatrics. I've waited more years than the grandfather of your grandfather lived, and I'm getting restless. Sometimes I wish Ms. Compton never let herself fall for you."

Whitmore looked pained at that comment. The women's voice was so nice and elegant, but I could tell that it was intended to hurt.

"You're right. I've also failed you, out of my own selfishness. Now is the time. No more mistakes." Whitmore says.

The woman's voice that came out of Whitmore spoke one more time.

"It's their turn, Ed. I hope you can make it right, or else the key might be in your own blood. And Scarlett knows what to do. Talk soon, Ed."

The ground starts to shake--a small earthquake, at just the right time? It only lasts a matter of seconds, and no one else seems to care or notice. This man is fucking crazy, but the women's voice is unexplainable.

Was Ed Whitmore just high and poisoned from the frog's venom? I didn't stop chanting, fearful Scarlett would do something else to Hayden. Why did he/she say, it was me that holds the key? I know what's going to happen. I'll be injected next, but not without a bargain. I need Hayden to get out of here. I can take whatever happens to me. I got everyone into this mess. This stupid YouTube video, this stupid serum. I cannot let Hayden die.

While I've been lost in my head about the inevitable, Whitmore falls to the ground and vomits up the red liquid.

"Get the vial with Parker's initials in on it. We can't waste any more time," Whitmore says, streams of blood running out of his nose from his violent heaving.

Scarlett heads down to the lab to collect the serum. I know I have only minutes to execute a plan.

Chapter 11

Seattle Washington 1993

I finally get out of the taxi that's pulled over on Campus Parkway. This is the first day of the rest of my life. At the beginning of the year, when I was still living in small-town Florida--and not even close to the ocean--with my mom, dad, and younger twin siblings, I never thought that I would step foot in the Pacific Northwest. I would come home every single day looking for that huge envelope that would contain my acceptance letter and welcome packet from the University of Washington. I never really dreamed of going to school all the way across the country, but UW developed one of the best robotics courses in the country, even standing up to the one at M.I.T.

I was always too smart for my tiny public school. They didn't have anything in the realm of robotics, but thankfully, I was able to attend robotics summer camps for all four years. Every year, I snagged the gold in our final projects, and that put me on the map. School scouts started calling our house every single night, driving my parents crazy. My first choice was M.I.T, but they refused to give me a full ride. That's when I finally got the full-ride offer from UW. Even though it's only their third year offering the program, I have high hopes that'll eventually land me my dream career.

I stroll across campus, taking in the giant fountain in the middle of the grounds surrounded by all the old architecture and scholarly buildings. The brisk breeze is announcing that fall is upon us, but the sun is still shining for now. I'm excited for the rain, even though everyone says I'll probably get tired of it. I finally get past the fountain and see a sign pointing in the direction of the dorms.

I head on my way and pop up the concrete stairs to my building and open the door. There's a person at the front desk checking everyone in, but the line was a mile long. I sneak on by, already knowing what room I've been placed in, and take the elevator to the third flood. I can get my keys later if I need to. I finally find my room, which is the one farthest away from the elevators but right next to the stairs. It'll give me a good excuse to maybe get some exercise, I think to myself as I look down at my small beer belly. There's nothing I love more than sitting down at my desk with metal, wires, a soldering iron and a cold beer.

I give one courtesy knock and a tall, skinny boy with dark shaggy hair opens the door. He pushes his black-rimmed glasses back up his nose and says, "Can I help you?"

"Yeah man, hey! My name is Edward Whitmore, but you can just call me Eddy. I'm your new roommate. You must be Alex?" I say as I offer my hand out for him to shake.

For a split second I think he's about to slam the door right back in my face. He looks me up and down, and then, all of a sudden, grabs my hand in a tight shake and pulls me in for a hug.

"Awesome! It's great to meet you, Eddy. The dude that was supposed to be my bunkmate last year dropped out after, like, the first week. I guess he couldn't handle the pressure. They felt bad for me last year not having a roommate and all. I guess it seems they let freshmen and sophomores bunk together. Well, hell yeah! I didn't even pass some of my gen eds, so maybe you could help me study! What're you studying? I'm going to be an electrical engineer!" Alex says, elbowing me in the ribs in a friendly manner.

"I'm here for the new robotics course they're offering," I say, still standing in the doorway.

"Oh shit, where are my manners, come on in and make yourself at home! There used to be a bunk bed, but I get claustrophobic, so I made them into two twin-sized beds on each side." Alex says with obvious pride.

The dorm room is probably one of the smallest rooms I've ever seen. I've never not had my own room, so the idea of sharing this extremely small one with Alex is making me a bit uneasy.

"I hope you don't snore, man," I say in a joking tone as I look over at his side of the room.

His walls are plastered with glossies of fancy cars like I would have had when I was 8 and Minnesota Twins posters.

"Oh yeah, you like my posters? I love baseball more than anything! Do you maybe wanna come to the pub with me and watch a game? I was actually just about to head out," Alex says.

"Maybe I can meet you there in a little bit? I want to unpack a little and at least get my bed made," I say.

"Yeah, for sure, I'll be at The Silver Dollar, and I might hit up this house party after the game. The frat house down the street usually goes a little crazy for new school year parties," Alex says.

"Sounds good man, it was super nice to meet you. I'll catch you at the Silver Dollar later," I say, smiling back at my first college friend.

Alex pretends to shoot me with finger guns and then blows the smoke off his finger tips on the way out the door. I try and sigh my nerves away and start unpacking. I stretch the navy blue sheet my mom bought me across my bed and hang some shirts up in our two-foot-long closet. Alex has already taken more than half the space for his things, but I don't mind. I've never been the type to have more than five shirts, two hoodies, and two pairs of pants.

I take another look around and see a tiny window with what I assume is Alex's mini fridge underneath. On the left and right side are two small desks. The one by Alex's bed is cluttered with books, paper, magazines and a few crumbs of marijuana here and there. I start neatly stacking my books on top of my own desk and start organizing all of my notebooks.

It's Friday night. I don't think I've ever been invited to an actual party in my entire life. I'm used to sitting at home reading Robotics Magazine and watching my mom and dad play cards. I sit up on my twin-sized mattress and decide to head out to the bar. The address, luckily, is circled in the phonebook with the words "Just two blocks!" written right next to it in scratchy handwriting. I assume this is Alex's favorite place, and he seems very proud of himself that he found it, or maybe his drunken self was just reminding his sober self of the gem he found. I throw on a dark grey plain hoodie and head out.

Once I'm outside, the rain is finally coming down. I hadn't had time to run to the store to grab an umbrella, and everyone I pass looks at me like I'm from another planet. The Silver Dollar turns out to be very easy to find with its bright blue neon sign reflecting off the puddles in the street. I walk in and shake out my longer-than-usual brown hair. I see Alex in the corner of the bar waving to me like he had been waiting for me to walk in.

I head over the table and see that Alex is sitting with another man.

"Hey, grab a pint and share some of this pitcher with us, it's just Rainer. Oh, and this is David!" Alex says.

David doesn't take his eyes off the TV. His hands are entangled in his short black hair, and he's peering out of his fingers in horror.

"Hey, it's nice to meet you." I say as I put out my hand to try and shake his.

David ignores me completely and just yells, "Fucking dammit, this team is horrendous."

"Don't mind him. He has like $200 bet on this game, and they're getting their asses kicked," Alex says, laughing at David. I take the seat next to Alex and pour myself a beer from the half-empty pitcher.

After the game is over, David starts to lighten up and accept that he just lost $200.

"Drinks are on you two motherfuckers now!" he says, laughing as I get up to head to the bar. I don't mind buying him a beer. I'm so over the moon about having new friends I'd buy them both five. After too many pints to count, Alex gets up and says, "Alright gang. Now it's time to head over to the fraternity and get ourselves some free beer, I'm running out of money."

"Don't we have to be friends with them or pledge ourselves to even get into this party? We obviously don't have any boobs to show them, either," David says.

I honestly couldn't stop laughing at him.

"We won't even be noticed, there's going to be so many people there! Come on, don't be a little pussy," Alex says.

"I'm down, let's go. If we get kicked out, whatever!" I say waving my pint in the air and then swallowing the remnants.

"Alright, it's only across from campus a block. We got this, guys. Let's go!" Alex gets up and stumbles out of the bar with his fist in the air like he's in a movie scene.

David is local to Washington and remembered to bring an umbrella.

"You two are like two lost foreigners. Didn't you read that the PNW is like the rainiest place in the whole country?" David says. "Just try and get under my umbrella, you dumbasses!"

Alex, David, and I both try to share one umbrella across the entirety of campus. I keep getting pushed out because Alex can barely walk in a straight line. The rain feels good on my head that's aching from drinking, anyways.

We finally walk up to the front steps and the party is booming. Alex is right, there's no way anyone is going to know we aren't apart of the frat since it looks like the whole school is here. We walk through the crowded house, witnessing plenty of drunk 20-year-olds playing beer pong, flip cup, you name it. I grab a beer from the keg in the living room that's bobbing in a tray of melted ice. I make my way to the kitchen to lean on the counter, just taking everything in. I guess this is what college life is going to be like, I think to myself.

I finish my beer and wander around the house looking for Alex. My head starts to throb as music and laughter fill the void. I can barely hear my own thoughts. I decide to walk outside to see if I could bum a smoke. I never smoke, but there's a first time for everything, right? I get outside to the porch to see people throwing up in the bushes and getting in their cars to, unfortunately, drive themselves home.

"Hey, you know you should've brought an umbrella?" says a girl's voice coming from the other side of the wooden front porch.

I suddenly notice my hair is still damp from the walk over. My eyes follow the voice to the most beautiful girl I've ever laid eyes on. She has dark curly hair with jeans hugging her belly button. Her dark brown skin and green eyes glow from under the moon and reflect perfectly off the Seattle rain.

"Yeah, you're right, I'm just a very unprepared person, I guess. Do you mind if I bum one of your cigarettes?" I say.

She reaches in her pocket and pulls out her pack, offering me one. I throw the white stick in my mouth as she lights it for me. The scent of her skin is intoxicating.

"Thanks. My name is Edward Whitmore, but you can just call me Eddy," I say to her politely.

"Nice to meet you, Eddy. My name is Jessica Compton, but you can just call me Jess," she responds, her lips curling up over her perfect white teeth into the most gorgeous smile I've ever seen.

"You know, I had a dream about this moment," she says.

"What do you mean? Like, this exact moment in time?" I say playfully.

"Yeah, you don't believe me?" she says.

"I don't know. I really didn't even have my night planned before my roommate begged me to come out and see what college life is all about," I say to her.

"Well, in my dream, you walk me back to my dorm," she says with a crooked smile. I wanted to go home anyway, and I'm definitely not dumb enough to say no to a girl as beautiful as her.

I put my left hand on my hip and offer her my arm. She takes it joyfully and opens her umbrella for the two of us. I gotta say, it fit us perfectly together.

"So where are you from Eddy, and what brought you to the rainiest place on earth?" Jess says to me.

"Well, I'm originally from a small town in Florida, but I came out here for the robotics program," I say.

"Smart man then, eh?" Jess says.

"I mean, I wouldn't call myself that smart. I just love robots and trying to build them. I think they are maybe going to take over the world, so I want them to remember who made them and maybe be a little grateful, enough to not kill me!" I say.

Jess smiles at my dumb joke and it makes me melt inside.

"What about you? What're you doing here?" I ask.

"I'm from just up north in Vancouver, Canada. I didn't really come here for school, but I thought a degree couldn't hurt, so I'm studying business," Jess says.

"What else did you come here for, besides the seafood?" I say.

"Well, that was a short walk, my dorm is right here," Jess says, stopping abruptly, ignoring the question and letting go of my arm. "Are you religious?" she says to me, after a short pause.

"Uh, no, I mean my grandparents went to church and stuff, but my parents never went with them and never baptized me or anything like that," I say.

"All you boys really just think of the small picture, don't you? Either Catholic or Buddhist or just Christian, whatever is the easiest God that will help all the white men and the white men just use it against everyone," Jess says.

"Woah, I mean I don't really believe in any of that, I'm open to whatever comes my way. I'm a college freshman, I need to expand my horizons!" I say with my arms up in the air and the rain falling on my face. I would literally say anything for this girl to like me.

"Well, if you say so, you should pick me up here Sunday morning at 10 am and I'll show you what you're missing," Jess says.

"It's a date!" I say to her with a goofy smile.

"Goodnight, Eddy," Jess says to me, and then she kisses me on the cheek. I'm in shock. I walk back to my dorm, again without an umbrella, but I don't mind. The goofy smile never leaves my face.

Saturday is a blur of finally getting checked in with the R.A. and mapping all my classes so I won't get lost on campus. With the robotics course, I unfortunately have to take a couple general ed classes that I'm really not looking forward to: Trig II, English I, and Psychological History. Fortunately, I also have two classes of robotics that I'm over the moon about.

After drinking a couple beers with Alex in my dorm room (immediately regretting them when I look down at my belly and wonder if Jess noticed how out of shape I am), I go to bed early for my date while Alex went back to the Silver Dollar.

I toss and turn all night long. At first, I think it's just anxious butterflies, but then soon realized it feels like my brain is vibrating. It felt like someone trying to put a key into an old rusty lock to force a stuck door open. All I can smell all night is rose pedals, the same intoxicating smell that hung around Jess. It's the only thing that gets me through the night.

I wake up the next morning feeling like a million bucks. My eyes shoot open and energy flows through my veins. I don't even want my usual burnt coffee from the pot my mom gave me before I left. *That's so fucking weird, I barely slept a minute*, I think to myself. I shrug it off, take a shower and get dressed. I head over to Jess's dorm.

On my way over, my armpits start sweating. I realize I don't even know what room she's in, and I obviously can't just walk into the building without living there. It's 10:01am when I approach her dorm.

"You're late," Jess says to me. She's standing outside on the dorm steps, smoking a cigarette. She has a light burnt orange rain jacket on with dark brown hiking pants, still as gorgeous as ever.

I laugh a little and say, "I'm sorry, please forgive me!" in the silliest voice I could muster. Today she doesn't laugh, but she does take my arm again as we walk towards the parking lot.

"You have a car?" I ask.

"Yeah, it's nothing much, though. I sold most of my stuff to come down here," Jess says.

We walked up to her red Jeep Liberty with light brown leather seats. I buckle my seatbelt and say, "So where's this date going to be, my lady?"

"You said you wanted to try everything. If you like it, I'll tell you everything afterwards. Please just do as I say and leave your mind completely open," Jess says to me as she puts her hand on my thigh.

We drive for about an hour into the woods making small talk about music and school. I can see her green eyes through the sides of her sunglasses as the Washington sun beams through the trees. The smell of roses makes my heart pump warm blood to my cheeks, making me blush. Her hand on my thigh is also making blood rush to other places.

"We're here," Jess says as we pull into a dirty driveway curling around tree after tree.

I can't see anything yet and begin to think—and maybe hope--that we're just going out on a picnic, maybe to her favorite spot.

"You're not, like, a serial killer, are you?" I say jokingly.

"Kinda too late to ask that in the middle of the forest, don't you think?" Jess says, throwing me another crooked smile.

The trees clear out into a clearing with a giant circus-like tent in the middle. Rope is nailed to the ground to keep the giant white sheet from flying off. I'm in awe. How is this huge place open in the middle of the forest with not even one sign around on the way in?

Jess pulls up in the dirt parking lot with painted white lines like a football field that's holding around 20 cars and puts the Jeep in park.

"What is this place?" I say, dumbfounded.

"This is the church of the Great Azazela," Jess says. "Come on, we're right on time."

We head toward the tent's opening and see men, women, children, families, you name it. Every kind of person is welcome here, it seems. As we walk through the big makeshift wooden doors, I'm greeted by a man who's holding one plastic cup with a blue liquid inside.

"A beverage before you sit, sir?" He says to me.

"Oh no thank you, it seems like there's only one left. I would be glad to give it to someone else," I say to him.

"Take it and drink it," Jess says to me. "It's only courtesy."

I take the cup, nodding my head in thanks to the man, and follow Jess down the aisle. The place is massive, with dark wooden pews scattered throughout the whole place. Up front where, if you went to Mass, you would see Jesus on a cross, there's a giant metal statue of a triangle on top of an upside-down triangle, with an x going right through both. Under the statue are bones mimicking the same shape.

"What the hell is that, Jess? Are those human bones?" I say, now starting to freak out a little bit.

"Don't worry about it, they aren't real," she says and winks her left eye.

We sit down in the second pew from the front as I start to sip on my drink. It tastes like a sports drink if someone threw some salt in it. I drink the whole thing to be polite.

It seems that as soon as we sit down, a priest of some sort in a billowing black gown with the triangle symbol stitched in red on the front walks up to the makeshift altar on the tent and stops by the metal statue.

"Thank you all for coming and celebrating this special day with us. The Great Azazela thanks you for your time and patience," the man says.

I start to get light-headed and the room begins to spin. I can barely hear what the man is saying, nor did I care. My mouth suddenly waters and before I know it, I'm holding in vomit. Beads of sweat drip down my forehead, and I brace myself on the pew in front of me.

"Jess, I don't feel very well," I whisper, trying not to make a scene in a church.

Jess ignores me and shuts her eyes.

"Let's begin," the priest says, and everyone in the tent starts chanting at once. It sounds like Latin, but I can't make out any words. My head spins so fast I lose my grip on the pew and fall out into the aisle.

Everyone is still chanting.

I'm on my hands and knees and, feeling stronger now that I'm grounded, finally look up. The bone on the ground starts shaking like there's an earthquake. I look around and everyone has their eyes closed. The ground underneath the triangle structure starts to split open, and the bones fall into the red glowing flames beneath the earth. The muted metal statue turns to bright gold as it shines so brightly in front of me that my eyes naturally squint.

What comes out of the ground is indescribable.

I can't decide if I'm seeing God or the Devil. The body is black and feathered but morphing into a triple helix with the most breathtaking skin I've ever seen. Its dozens of eyes glittered in a spectrum of color that never existed before in my universe. Suddenly, I feel embraced, with nothing or no one touching me. Warm like when my mother held me skin to skin when I was a baby. A scene none of us get to remember, but this creature is pouring it into my head. The feeling was better than all the drugs, all the sex in the entire universe. Suddenly looking upon, her I felt my purpose. I felt any worry in my veins run and hide. I feel safe, content.

The creature opens my mind and I finally let go. I'm in a white room with a black shadowed women. I know everything. She tells me everything. Azazela. I'm speaking to her. I'm her chosen vessel. Jess brought me here because Azazela came into her dreams. This was the plan all along. They knew every step I was going to take, and finally, I was here. Finally, my path in life has been chosen.

"I will do everything in my power to help you. I will put my life on the line to follow your greatness. We will own the world," I say to her.

"Good," Azazela says to me in the most angelic tone of voice you could ever imagine.

"Take Jess's hand in marriage, get up and kill the priest. It's his time to go. You two are now the vessels of me," Azazela says.

"How will they know to follow me?" I ask.

Azazela curls her pure black silhouetted hand over my cheek and says, "You will be the first one to meet me in the white room without going back and throwing up your intestines until you suffocate. I have great plans and intentions for you, Edward Whitmore."

CHAPTER 12

Seattle, Washington: 3 Years Later

"I just don't know what else to do, we can't fucking kill everyone. I know the sacrifices are working and Azazela is pleased for now, but I need a better option," I say to Jess as I pace back and forth in our brand-new condo under the Seattle Space Needle that the church pitched in to buy their leader. "Law enforcement is going to start noticing all these missing people in the PNW and start asking questions."

Jess sighs and rubs her belly while sitting at the kitchen table.

"Baby, come here, she's kicking," Jess says to me as I put my breakfast down (over easy eggs with bacon) and hurry over. I place my hand on her protruding stomach, still smelling nothing but roses like the day we met. I feel a tiny foot hit my hand right over her belly button. I smile and lay my head on her shoulders breathing in her scent and letting her take all of my frustrations away.

"You know, Azazela might've told me to marry you, but I was in love with you from the very moment you made fun of me not having an umbrella my first night in town," I say to Jess.

"I know, Eddy, you tell me that quiet often. I love you so much, and I'm sure Scarlett is going to love her daddy just as much as I do," Jess says. "We will figure this out. We still are slowly building her army, one by one. The sacrifices and the rituals are going flawlessly, and I doubt the police are racing to our secret neck of the woods."

Literally our neck of the woods. Jess is right; I don't think anyone knows about our little white circus tent an hour outside of town in the middle of the forest. The only people that know are people who have dedicated their lives to Azazela.

If someone in our community wants another to join, they have to go through a strenuous process. First, I meet them outside of the church. We go on a little coffee date or grab a beer. Once I've ran a multitude of background checks and know for certain they aren't trying to unravel my entire plan--everyone's plan--of world domination for Azazela, they have to commit to a blood oath.

We take them to the church, blindfolded. They bow down to the Great Azazela and speak the words of our ancient Latin language. Everyone surrounds them, standing on the bones of our sacrifices. I take a violently hot brand of Azazela's symbol of mind control. Both triangles are a foot long and the x going over them will hit both of your shoulder blades down to the very top of the buttocks. If they survive the pain and dance around the infection from the healing skin, that leaves just one more task: they will have to bring someone to the church for a sacrifice.

I don't give a shit if they're drugged and thrown in the trunk of a car or simply just lied to. They can tell them it's the best fucking carnival they've ever seen. Tell them about the bearded lady and the tightrope walkers. They'll come and be given to Azazela. Every week, we have a new sacrifice. Even if we don't have a fresh face to get our sacrifices here, we all take turns bringing them. All take turns showing our commitment to our cause.

"Alright, baby, eat your breakfast and let's get out of here and head to the woods," Jess says as she slicks my dark brown hair back out of my eyes.

"Oh, but do we have to go today? Let's call in sick and lay in bed, maybe fool around a bit," I say with a sly smile on my face while walking behind her to massage her shoulders.

"You're such a little shit. We run this church, and we need to be there every Sunday. I think it was Ann's turn to bring the sacrifice, her first one," Jess says.

"I know, I know," I say with a huge frown on my face, but I can't keep it up without laughing with Jess and giving her a small kiss on the lips.

We get in the car and start driving towards the moss-covered trees. It's late October. The fog is creeping through the tree lines like smoke, obscuring the faint sunbeams peaking from behind the clouds. I'm still working on my robotics degree, anticipating graduating early. The generosity of the people in the church let us have a house over our head and food on the table. They know that Azazela had picked me, and they would do their very best to support our every need. Jess dropped out of school once we became pregnant with Scarlett.

God, I can't wait till she's born into this amazing world of ours. I reach out and turn on the country station as we drive down the deserted highway. I guess there's no home football game today, thank the Great Azazela. I notice Jess start to get uneasy in her seat. She starts moaning and whispers a little "What the fuck?" while she curls over her belly and holds it in her hands.

"Jess, are you okay? What's happening?" I say to her, still trying to keep my eyes on the road.

"I think I'm okay, they might just be false contractions. We aren't due for another 6 weeks so I can't be going into labor, right?" Jess says through the pain.

"Well, you very well might be, do you want me to go to the hospital? I can pull over and..."

She stops me in my tracks and says, "Eddy, calm down. It's okay. I think I'm okay. Maybe it was just some heartburn or something. Let's get to the church."

"Okay, but if something doesn't feel right any second of the rest of the day, you have to tell me, promise?" I say to Jess as I take one hand off the wheel to hold one of hers.

"Yes, I promise," Jess says and squeezed my hand back.

We both get out of the car and see the giant wooden doors already swung open for us. We walk in hand in hand, smiling and shaking hands with everyone greeting us. While we walk down the wide aisle to the Azazela's statue, Jess takes her seat in the "wife's throne," as we call it, and I stand while everyone starts to settle down in their pews. I wait until everyone is sitting, trying to meet eyes with Ann and her sacrifice. She hasn't emailed me or mentioned anything about who or how she's bringing them, but I trust her. She went through her initiation well, even when her husband left her with their small boy. I notice everyone take their seats and smile directly at me. I've led a sermon now every Sunday for the last three years. My nerves went away fast, and everyone took me in as their own as their master. The vessel, some of them will call me, but it tickles them I call them vessels back.

"Good morning, my vessels! Today is going to be a wonderful day celebrating the Great Azazela. Yet again, she hasn't visited us in our dreams this week, but that must mean we're on the right path and doing great with our worshiping," I say loudly to my group. Everyone cheers and claps.

"This week, we have Ann's second dawn! Let's all give Ann a welcoming clap."

Everyone claps one time while Ann stands up in the back pew.

Ann starts walking towards me with her small son's hand in hers. She's a white-and grey-haired lady with stone-washed jeans and a puffy black vest jacket on. She looks like she could be the boy's grandma, but she was only pushing her late 30s. The boy has short black hair, can't be older than 5. He's also wearing a small black puffy jacket and jeans. They march right up to me, and the boy let go of her hand.

"Ann, where's your sacrifice? I'm not letting you hurt your boy," I say to her, out of earshot of the churchgoers.

Instead of answering me, Ann turns around to face the crowed and says, "Azazela hasn't come to Edward, but she came to me earlier this week in a dream."

The churchgoers gasp and I think to myself that this can't be real. No words come out of my mouth.

Ann starts again, "The Great Azazela told me I was her sacrifice. She needs me with her. I didn't bring anyone here today for the ritual because I am the ritual!"

Ann turns to look at me and says, "Please, Edward, take my boy. You're already starting a family. He needs you, and you're the only one I trust."

"No, Ann, this is not how it's supposed to go…" I say reaching out to her. Before I can take another step, Ann pulls out a pistol, puts it to her head and says, "Hail the Great Azazela!" and pulls the trigger.

Blood splatters onto the front stage left side of the pews as people gasp and talk. Some run out to wash the blood off their face and some just sit and bask in the sacrifice, wishing Azazela came to them in their dreams.

The boy walks over to his mom's body.

"Mommy please wake up. Please." He starts crying as Jess walks over to the boy, bends down and rubs her hand through his hair in a comforting motion.

"It's okay son, your mommy is in a better place with a greater purpose than here. She's with Azazela, honey."

The boy hugs onto Jess as she starts to stand up. I'm completely in shock. This isn't how it's supposed to happen. There's no way Azazela came to Ann before talking it over with me. I feel betrayed. Maybe Ann's just fucking crazy, killing herself to make a spectacle.

I feel a bead of sweat drip down the side of my face. I stare at the people in the pews as they stare back at me, waiting for me to address them. They're all just like Ann. Maybe Azazela did come to her just to make me jealous. All these people are here just to make me jealous. A copper taste fills my mouth as my teeth clench down onto my own tongue.

As soon as Jess pulls another chair up to the "wife's throne" for the boy, she falls over and lets out a deafening scream. She hunches over onto her knees, hands clutching the bones at the front of the so-called church.

I run over to her as fast as I can and say, "We're going to the hospital."

I stand up and feel the boy take my hand. I don't have time for this. The love of my life could possibly be dying. We never should have come here today.

I stand up and shout, "Help me carry her to my car!"

Some men in the second row that think of me as their friend whose names I wouldn't be able to tell you walked calmly over and picked up Jess as she was still screaming. Blood now covered her pants and dripped down the inside of her thighs. Before I knew it, she's in the front seat of our same old Jeep Liberty and I'm flying down the highway to the nearest hospital. In the rearview mirror, I see the boy looking blankly out the window, the sun making his eyes squint.

The waiting room is blindingly white and two people in blue scrubs are speaking to me.

"Did you hear me, Mr. Whitmore?" the chubbier one is saying to me. I can feel the small boy's head resting against my shoulder while he slept soundly.

"I'm sorry, what do you mean?" I say to them in a hoarse voice.

"Mr. Whitmore, your wife delivered a premature but healthy baby girl. Jessica had extreme bleeding. We couldn't stop it in time, and with your wife's rare blood type, we couldn't get any from the Seattle hospital fast enough. We did everything in our power. I'm very sorry for your loss." the surgeon says.

Everything inside me dropped. I was holding back puke. My hands and legs went numb, and I swear everyone was smiling at me.

"We'll give you a moment, but your baby is ready to see you when you're able," The other surgeon says as they start to walk away to maybe just fucking kill someone else's wife.

My legs are paralyzed and my ass is glued to the chair. There is a discolored tile in the floor to the left of my foot. I wish I knew how long I stared at it for.

Scarlett had to stay in the hospital for a month, and so did the boy and I. He was a good kid, my little buddy. He would do anything for me, even though his mom just shot herself in the head mere days ago. Scarlett looks just like her mom, with downy brown hair and green eyes. The most beautiful baby I've ever seen. I thanked the Great Azazela that she had none of my features and just Jess's perfection. The little girl even smelled of roses.

When we finally got to go home, I thought I would be overwhelmed having two small children, but the boy's brain was older than his years. He helped his sister, he helped me, even when every single thing in my life reminded me of Jess. Some days, the boy would take on all responsibility in the house while I internally cried for my lost wife. I never blamed any of it on Scarlett, though. She was my light. She was standing in the footprints of her mother, and I knew she would be great.

I had no idea what was going on in the church or if they were even continuing our rituals, our rules. They kept paying for the house and sending me money to help with the baby, but no one came to visit. I liked it that way, anyway.

After six weeks of being absent from church and home with the children, I wake up early, thankful everyone was still fast asleep so I could have a second of quiet. I head down the winding stairs of our condo, which I guess is just my condo now, to grab a cup of coffee. Next to the coffee maker is a small glass jar with a cork in it. The contents of the cup are a light blue color. There's a note with handwriting that looked extraordinarily like Jess's. The note says "drink me."

What the hell do I have to lose, I think to myself. *The children probably don't need me, hell, Azazela probably doesn't need me anymore, either.* I take the cup and drink the contents. It tasted just like it did three years ago, a sports drink mixed with extra salt this time around.

"I'm fucking done with your self-pity Edward," Azazela says to me in the white room. "Jess is safe, it was her destiny to come meet me here, you're brave for taking on both children and they will become essential to you and your will."

My heart flutters. The feeling of Jess's kisses and hugs, her smell, that intoxicating voice are all felt when Azazela is here.

"I'm deeply sorry, my queen, I never meant to question your plan for me, it's just been so hard. Do you think I could see Jess, just to see if she's okay?" I say to her, tears piercing my eyes.

"Your journey is not going to get any easier, Edward, this is just the beginning, but since you're at a standstill, I've found greater purpose elsewhere. You don't believe my words that Jess is with me and finally at peace?" Azazela says, taking a step back from me.

"No! What do you mean? I'm here for good. Please, I'll do whatever it takes. I know this was Jess' wish, and I will teach the kids about her and you, and we will all be your golden vessels. I promise!" I plead.

"I'll give you one more chance, Edward Whitmore. Kill the whole congregation this Sunday. Take our small vessels and move out of this place," Azazela says to me.

The boy and I packed up all our stuff a couple days before Sunday's ritual. We throw clothes, toys, pictures, even my old college textbooks into the moving boxes. I've looked up places where the sun shines but has every season. I want Scarlett to have the most perfect childhood. Denver, Colorado came up on one of my searches, and I learned it has over 300 days of sunshine a year. It was far enough away from our life in Seattle, and I read they just opened a whole technical center focusing on the future. I'm sure I could get a robotics job there, where I'll still be able to teach my kids about Azazela and hopefully do some more of my own rituals.

When Sunday arrives, we drive up to the giant white circus tent one last time. It would be Scarlett's first and last time as part of this congregation. I walk in smiling, and for a second, everyone is shocked. The next, they all welcome me back with open arms and give me my rightful place in front of the giant statue to lead today's ritual.

"Hello, my fellow vessels! I'm so glad to be back in your presence. Today, we are going to do something truly special to welcome my family back," I yell to the crowed.

Everyone is so cheerful and happy, chapping and yelling, "Thank you, Great Azazela!"

I gesture to the boy to start pouring blue liquid into see-through plastic cups.

"Today, the Great Azazela is going to visit everyone! Today we are all going to drink the great potion of her will. We will all visit the white room!" I yell.

People gasp in shock.

"Come on up and grab yourself a cup, no one is excluded, and everyone must drink to share the experience," I say, even though I know everyone is over the moon about sharing this sacred drink with each other.

Everyone files up to the front, one by one like a communion line. Once all the men, women and children have each acquired their cup, I hold mine to the roof of the white tent with both hands and say, "Great Azazela, let us all join you in the white room! Now, everyone drink!"

The congregation chugged everything, every last drop, out of each transparent cup.

It didn't take long for the blood to start streaming from their noses. The screaming starts. People are lying on their sides, vomiting up blue mixed with red blood, clenching their stomachs. Some run off into the woods, but I knew they wouldn't get far before the poison enters their blood stream. White and red foam spill out of their ears as each one of them dies a painful death. I watch as the people in front of me die one by one, thinking I'm Azazela's vessel, I am the chosen one. All these people are nothing to me. I also was very grateful for taking Psychological History freshman year, when I met Jess, for the inspiration. I take Scarlett out of her seat and carry her to the moving van with the boy right behind me. We step over bodies on our way out.

My new job in Denver pays the perfect amount for the kids and I to get a house and live as a happy family. The years fly by, and Scarlett is now 23 and as beautiful as ever. Looking exactly like her mom still.

I wish Jess could see the women she's turned into; she would be so proud. The boy is in his late 20s, I think, but I had always guessed at his age. He's quiet and likes to do things alone. He's helped me through everything and is always by my side, never once complaining or questioning. They both learn about Azazela and how they are her golden vessels. We each do our own sacrifices once a month.

The boy and I would kill on our own terms, but Scarlett has a different approach. She meets men on the internet and start dating them and then takes their body and minds as sacrifices. It's all fun and games to her, but I know that deep down inside, she knows why she was doing this. Azazela hasn't come to us in over 20 years, but I still try and figure out how to make the world hers every single day.

One afternoon, I came home from work with a surprise. Scarlett and the boy were sitting on the couch, she on her phone and he reading a book (they were both going crazy during quarantine).

"Hey guys, so my work is going out of business, but do you remember how I told you about the AI robots we were creating?" I say.

Scarlett barely looked up from her phone and nodded her head, the boy looked at me and says "Yeah."

"Well, I stole the serum we put in the robots. They had this serum running through their veins instead of a chip controlling their commands."

"What're you getting at, Dad?" Scarlett says, now interested in what was in my hand.

"What if it works on humans?" I say. "If it worked, we could stop killing humans for Azazela and start building her army on earth with mind control."

"We have to try it, I volunteer. This is my purpose," The boy says, standing up.

"No, this is my purpose! Dad, you know I was the chosen child with mom, he is just here because you had to take him in!" Scarlett whines.

"Don't say that to your brother, he has done nothing but help this family all these years. Besides, it's my choice, and I think the boy is right," I say.

"Thank you, sir. I'm ready now," the boy says.

Scarlett has always been a hothead when she doesn't get her way. I feel awful, but if something were to go wrong, I would rather it go wrong in the boy's body than hers. I need her. I take the syringe out of the metal suitcase and pull the fluid up into it. Its silver spirals are hypnotizing.

"On three."

"No, just do it, sir," they boy says calmly.

I take a deep breath for the sake of my own sanity and inject the serum into his neck. The boy just sits back down on the couch and takes his legs, pulls them toward his chest and then sticks his thumb in his mouth like a toddler.

"Hi mommy!" he says.

"What the fuck is happening?" Scarlett whispers to me.

"I don't know, honestly," I say.

"Should we ask him to do something? What's the first thing that comes to mind?" Scarlett says to me.

I can hear the boy laugh and giggle at his invisible mom playing peek-a-boo.

"Hey boy, go make me a sandwich now!" I try and say with as much authority and assertion as I can muster.

The boy gets up and says, "Yes, Mommy," and goes in the kitchen to make me a sandwich.

"It worked," I say, in shock and trying to ignore the fact that the boy saw right through me to his mom.

Chapter 13

"Please, I'll do anything. Just let Hayden go," I plead to Whitmore.

Scarlett comes back up the stairs with the vial encasing the silver swirly liquid. Whitmore ignores me while he makes sure there are no air bubbles in the tube of the syringe, spraying small drops of liquid on the floor. *There's no plan,* I think to myself as Hayden's eyes fall further and further into their sockets. *I don't know what to fucking do.*

"Did you by chance check on the boy downstairs?" Ed Whitmore says.

"Yeah, I peeked into his shit room. He's still watching SpongeBob with his 'mommy'" Scarlett says with her fingers in the air once again.

I turn to Scarlett, with no hope left, and say, "Please Scarlett, just let Hayden go. For Jameson at least. We were all best friends."

Scarlett starts to laugh and says, "Yeah right, you fucking idiot. Jameson was just another one of my games. He was cute and all, but this is bigger than all of us."

"Don't amuse them, Scarlett, Azazela is getting tired of us already. I can tell by the feeling in my gut." Ed Whitmore says.

"What do you mean, he's with his mom? What the hell did you guys do to him?" I say, trying to buy more time before the needle hits my neck.

Ed considers explaining, and his ego takes the better of him.

"Well, Parker, since this could be the end of you and all, I might be able to explain a small fraction of our work," he says.

"You see, I injected that boy three years ago with the same serum your little girlfriend helps make. It took to him very well. Instead of transporting his brain into a whirlwind of fucked up past memories and the injection causing him to refuse commands, his brain took him to his best memories. With his mom. Now he thinks he's about five years old again, taking orders from the person in his life that he loved the most. His brain can still process all he's learned in his adult life, too. That's why he could carry on a conversation with you while handing you the mystery box at your apartment complex. He also was the one standing outside your apartment warning you both you only had one more day to see me." Ed Whitmore explains proudly.

"Then why not do experiments on him and figure out why the serum isn't working on other people in your expensive ass lab?" I yell as I see Ed getting ready to stab my neck.

Hayden is still next to me, looking like she's taking it all in, but she still needs to go to the hospital. Her eyes are receding into her skull, and it makes me sick to my stomach looking at the love of my life like this.

"He's still my boy, Parker. I'm tired of explaining this to you. It's not worth my time. After the injection, we hope you'll turn out like him, but if you don't, all this effort won't just be wasted. You'll all just be my sacrifice of the month, instead," Ed Whitmore says with a small sigh.

With my hands still tied tightly behind my back, Ed Whitmore comes up to me and takes my chin between his pointer finger and thumb. He moves my neck slightly to the left like

Hayden used to do when she was kissing me. Soon after that I felt something like ice cubes enter my veins, and Whitmore pulls back with an empty syringe in his hand.

I wake up in my two-bedroom apartment in Eastern Denver in a cold sweat shirtless in bed. Hayden is still fast asleep next to me while Boba curls up in between her legs. He looks up worried at my sudden waking with the blanket gripped between both of my fists. I catch my breath and start wondering what the fuck even happened? Where are Whitmore and Scarlett and why are we in my bed in my apartment?

I glance around the room and realize that the TV is hanging on the wrong wall and our bed is now facing the window. When the hell did we rearrange? Boba starts licking his paws and I see that the dark brown eyebrows he used to have are now gone. Or did he even have them in the first place? I get an uneasy feeling that I'm going crazy. This feels like my house, my safe space, but it doesn't look quite right.

Hayden wakes up, rolls over and reaches for my arm. "Hey, baby, what're you doing up so early? We don't have any videos to shoot today, it's our weekend."

"What do you mean? What happened with the mystery box?"

"Parker, you had a bad dream. We haven't even received the box yet."

"Parker's still lucid, it actually might be working," Whitmore says.

"When do you think we should ask them the question?" Scarlett says.

"I really don't know. The boy started talking right away, and ever since we've obviously failed with everyone else." Whitmore says, starting to sound anxious. Whitmore snaps his fingers in front of Parker's eyes, but they never blinked once.

Hayden now has me in her arms, and it feels better than it's ever felt before. The smell of roses blossoms off her neck. The warmth of her skin radiates heat into my soul. She kisses me on the forehead, and it feels like she's drained the worried feeling that's coursed through my nerves my entire life. It feels like jumping into the pool on a sweltering hot day, or bundling up next to the fire on Christmas Eve, looking at the tinsel on the tree. This felt better than all the sex and money in the world.

"Mhmm, Hayden," Parker whispers and they stare right at the wall past the statue.

"It's time, I think it's working. The boy has his mom to listen to, and Parker has their 'Hayden'" Whitmore says while he copies his daughter and moves his fingers up and down with air quotes.

"I told you, Scarlett, that I would let you be the one to start it and be the voice of the control. Now, ask them the simple question,"

Scarlett looks at her dad with loving eyes and reaches down to cut off Parker's ties.

"Thank you, Dad. I will not let Azazela down." Scarlett reaches into her pocket, takes out the Home Depot multitool and flicks the blade open.

"Parker, kill her."

"What the hell are you doing?" Whitmore yells.

"Put your hand in my chest and take out my heart," Hayden says to me grabbing my hand. I'm confused at this gesture. Nothing is making sense.

"It's all going to be okay. I'm going to be with you forever now," Hayden kisses me again on the forehead.

If this is what heroin feels like the first time you shoot up, call me a fucking addict. I put my fingers against her chest, gently at first, then push hard through the cavity of her sternum, reaching through all the blood pooling out by the sides of my hand. My hand goes in too smooth, like it's made of metal. I put my fingers around her heart and pull it out of her skin. Ventricles tear, but the heart in my hand keeps beating when fully removed. Hayden just smiles at the sight.

"The serum has taken over Parker completely," Whitmore says in awe as Hayden's lifeless body falls onto the pew.

Her hands and feet are still tied up with rope. Dark red is starting to stain the already disgusting floor. Parker's sitting next to her, knife in hand, blood running down to their elbow. Parker is staring at the knife now, smiling with their perfectly straight teeth.

"Wasn't this more fun, Dad? I learned all my theatrics from you!" Scarlett says with an evil laugh and ugly smile painted on her face.

Ed Whitmore wasn't amused by his daughter.

"Get this cleaned up. You're in charge of Hayden and Jameson's bodies. Cut their ear and toes off. Put them in the fridge. I don't give a shit where you bury the rest of the bodies, but I will not take no for an answer and you will obey me. I need to start running tests as soon as possible."

Scarlett knew her wit was definitely not welcome in this moment and that her dad was pissed, even though a miracle that hasn't happened in three years just occurred.

"I'll start with Jameson," Scarlett says quietly and goes down the stairs.

Whitmore follows Scarlett downstairs to grab hair clippers from the lab.

"Cut off all your hair."

"You know what you should do, baby? You should buzz your hair off," Hayden says to me with a giggle. There's a hole in her chest and blood is still trickling out, but none of it is leaking onto the bedsheets. It's like the blood is disappearing right as it's about to fall.

"I don't know, I think I'll just look exactly like my dad bald," I proclaim as I'm yet again starting to feel confused.

"It'll be so hot." Hayden says, as she grabs my inner thigh.

Days pass by while Whitmore cuts and prods at Parker down in the lab. Looking at blood and brain samples over and over again, trying to figure out why the serum is working on them. Nothing comes to fruition. Whitmore does worry about affecting Parker's brain with the experiments, but nothing ever happens. They practice with commands, chores, and math problems that they do on paper to make sure nothing bad is happening to Parker's brain. Making robots is a lot like the human body, but Whitmore is no surgeon.

Parker does every single thing Whitmore asks of them with no hesitation or complaint. Parker barely talks besides a "Yes, Hayden" or "Yes, my love" after getting commands, and Whitmore puts them in the room to share with the boy, chains and all. Neither notices the other one is there. Parker never looks directly into anyone's eyes and their eyes are always fixated on something that isn't there. Whitmore knows it's Hayden, but not her real spirit. That was given to Azazela.

We spend days in bed, Hayden and I. She asks me to do simple things like close my eyes and help her with her math homework. I didn't realize she was taking college classes again, and the equations seem easy, but I love helping her. We never get hungry in this room, and we never leave. Boba doesn't even have to eat, drink, or go outside, he's content just with us. I never question any of it because the feeling is too extraordinary. She has me lie on my stomach and tells me to be brave. I don't know why I have to be brave when all she is doing is rubbing the tips of her fingers up and down my back. Going from my butt all the way to my shoulder blades. I believe this is heaven, and Hayden is my one true god.

Whitmore has Parker lying prone in the dining room under the fake gun trap. Scarlett is holding their shoulders down in place, but Parker doesn't notice.

"Hold them still, it's going to fucking hurt, but Azazela will be pleased with the markings. We used to do this back in Washington to welcome new members. Parker is definitely a new member."

Whitmore fires up a propane torch and starts burning a metal brand in the shape of one triangle, one upside-down triangle and a cross going right through both. The metal gets placed on Parker's back from their buttocks right up to their shoulders. The skin melts and smokes, and it smells of cooking oxidized steak.

"Put them back in the room with the boy and chain their leg to the wall. They're both too special to us now to risk an escape. We will keep tabs on them with the camera on the wall."

Each night, when Hayden and Boba fall fast asleep in my arms, the darkness of my room encompasses one red light in the corner of the ceiling. Before I drift off, I can't help but stare.

"What do we do now, Dad?" Scarlett says.

"We make sure Parker heals and continue her will."

CHAPTER 14

"Hey there queers! And also straights, we love you too!" I say with my partner Brooklyn while we start filming the introduction to our newest YouTube video.

"My name's Kai and, as you all probably know, this is my beautiful partner Brooklyn, and we welcome you to the newest video on LGBTube, 'The Mystery Box'!" I say as Brooklyn presses a noise action button of a spooky laughing sound.

Brooklyn takes over and says, "I know you might've heard that our biggest competition, Put Up or Shut Up, came up with the idea first and I want to say we thought it was a great idea, and we were never going to steal it!"

"But!" I start to say, "It's been over a year since they put out that introduction video, and they've never posted a follow-up. We've tried to reach out to see what happened to the rest of the video with no response."

Brooklyn hops back in again, loudly. You can hear her echo from the high vaulted ceilings of her parent's house.

"Sooooo, we reached out to Whitcom industries and they emailed us back! They said that Parker and Hayden never reached back out, and they think they took the money and ran. I mean, it was $500,000, but that's very criminal of them."

"So, to keep this short and sweet, in honor of them either giving up, stealing the money, or dying..." I start to say as

Brooklyn cuts me off unscripted, "Don't say they died; that's not cool at all, Kai. A mystery box is scary enough."

"I know, it's just that I want the audience to think of how scary it is, too, we need more views on this video so we can actually get monetized and start making actual money. We talked about this. With the Put Up or Shut Up channel out of the way, we can finally be the number one queer channel on the internet," I say, turning off the camera.

"You're right, I'm sorry. It's just… what if something actually happened to them? What if they actually got the mystery box and something really, really bad happened to them?"

I start to laugh a little bit, but I promise, not at Brooklyn. She's just such a worrier, and she's concerned about people that have been our greatest competition during this entire career we're trying to start. She's one of those heroes that would never kill the bad guy, and it would always come back to haunt her.

"Wouldn't there be missing person reports on the internet we could look up? There's literally no trace of them, no paper trail. They had to have just conned Whitcom Industries and took off with the money, like they said. Let's pause for today and go to the beach, maybe have a beer?"

Brooklyn smiles and says, "Okay, well, the box is supposed to be here tomorrow. We might as well celebrate a little tonight. Let me edit this video on my phone real quick, and I'll put it up on our channel."

I don't have any family. I was an orphan growing up bouncing around different homes being thrown in and out of the system. I met Brooklyn at a bar here in town. She came up to me while I was sloppy drunk and asked if she could buy me a beer. I told her a shot and a beer and we had a deal. I don't know what she saw in me, for I'm not quite a looker. I have dyed blondish silver hair that's all spiked up like I haven't changed my style since the 2000s. I always wear the same black skinny jeans and ripped up shirts. I also have a thing for rings, and not just the ones that go on your fingers. I think she more saw my lost soul and wanted to help. We started hanging out after that first night, and eventually she got her rich parents to let me crash with them. While they might be filthy rich, they only let Brooklyn sleep in their house. They expect her and me to come up with our own money and start making a life for ourselves. Their house, though, is only about a 5-minute walk from the beach.

I follow Brooklyn down a path that we both know by heart. San Diego, California is perfect in the evening. The sun is setting over the ocean, but reflecting off her golden eyes. She has long red hair like her mom, almost see through now that the sun is making the clouds pink. She has freckles all over her face and arms. I think she's beautiful and fun, but I don't think we're really in love. It makes me sad because we're such a perfect fit, and the feelings of safety and longevity are something I can associate with her any day, but love is still foreign to us both.

We both bring two six-packs of White Claw with us to the beach and drink all of them between the two of us. We end up a little tipsy while we talk about our video. Whitcom says the mystery box is supposed to come bright and early tomorrow morning, so we won't waste any time pressing record and opening the box. We never were really good with being scripted.

"Look, Kai! Our intro video we finished earlier is already over a million views! If this mystery box opening gets a million more, we're on our way to making some money and moving out on our own!" Brooklyn says.

I don't really feel like moving out of her parents' house just yet, but I know she's dying to get our own place near LA. She says that's where all the famous YouTube stars live.

I give her such a big hug that she yelps a little bit, the air escaping her lungs a little too quickly, and say, "Yes! We're definitely on our way! I cannot wait for tomorrow!" We stagger home, make sloppy love and fall asleep.

I wake up feeling better than I should, and thank God, because we are supposed to be filming the video today. It's ten a.m., and I go to pour myself a cup of black coffee from the bland coffee pot right next to the espresso machine Brooklyn's parents have. It must've cost more than I've ever had in my pockets my entire life. Brooklyn's parents are usually out early and barely come home until late at night. Always at the country club, on yachts, or an expensive wine tasting. Her dad is CEO of a huge company I've never heard of, but I think it's in tech. The doorbell rings so I check my door camera app on my phone, and it looks like a man with a package! The man is wearing UPS brown and holding what looks like a brown colored package with small stains all around it. I rush to the door to greet the man.

When I open the door, I immediately say, "Thank you so much, I really needed this package early today!"

The person responds, "Is this 1358 Morrison Lane?"

"Well, it's Morrison Lane, but not those numbers, I was expecting a package, though."

"Oh yeah, this is for you. My mistake."

I notice that the person in front of me is wearing UPS brown, but I can't see any logo placed anywhere. They're kind of dirty, and I wonder how they let them come to work like that. I see that the patch on their clothes has a name tag on it -- sewn in white letters, I see the name: Parker.

My stomach drops, but this obviously can't be *the* Parker, can it? Their eyes were concaved a bit into their skull, but the bags under their eyes couldn't be missed. I couldn't see any hair underneath the brown baseball cap, and their skin looked like this is the first time they've seen the sun all year long.

"Well, I hope you have a great rest of your day. Have fun with the box!" They say as they walk back across the street. I can't see a mail truck anywhere on the street. All that's parked outside in this neighborhood are fancy cars and trucks being washed; no one usually parks their precious cars on the street. I see Parker walk to a red Jeep Liberty, start the engine and drive off.

I close the door, head back upstairs to our filming room and set the box on the table. It's a big box that can barely fit in my arms, and I have to rest my chest on the top to keep it from falling back down the stairs. The problem with that is that it smells worse than anything I've ever smelled before in my life. I set it down on our table and just stare at the stains darkening the corners.

I can hear Brooklyn brushing her teeth in the hall bathroom. She finishes and comes out saying, "What the fuck, did we roll in a sewer last night? Kai, you smell..." and then she sees the box, inviting her eyes in and then locking them in place.

"You'll never guess who delivered it," I say, still looking at the box.

"Who?"

"Parker."

"No fucking way, how do you even know?"

I pull out the Ring camera app on my phone and press the "Recent" tab. The doorbell camera is placed higher up, so we can only really see the top of the brown baseball cap they were wearing. They were also wearing long sleeves and gloves so we couldn't even see tattoos.

"Well, this doesn't prove anything" I say, frustrated. "I swear to you, Brooklyn, they had a patch sewn into their shirt with the name Parker, but their eyes were caved in, and they were so skinny and pale. They looked kind of like the Parker on the Put Up or Shut Up YouTube page, but this coincidence is freaking me out."

Brooklyn sits down next to me and says, "It's okay, I believe you. Let's just keep it out of the video for now. We have a show to shoot, so let's just get ready and start setting up to open this box, okay? Now is as good of a time as any!" She kisses my cheek, gets up and heads to the shower.

We both only take about 30 minutes to get presentable and to set up multiple cameras for different angles around the room. I press the record button on all of them except the handheld one and they all flash their red record lights right at us.

"Okay, I'll start. Are you ready, baby?" I say.

Brooklyn nods and I open our video with, "Hey queers and straights and everyone in between! Welcome to our channel LGBTube and our mystery box opening video! Just so you know, Whitmore Industries is sponsoring this video with a donation of over $500,000, and they helped us get the mystery box from the spooky dark web!"

Brooklyn chimes in and says, "We're prepared with gloves and face masks, so we don't get hurt with anything in here. But let's not keep these folks waiting, and let's start opening the box!"

We take a knife to the tape on top of the box, and the smell hits us like a semi-truck driving 100 mph down an icy hill.

"You go first," Brooklyn says as I reach my hand in and pull out a baby blanket with blood creeping down the face of Snow White. It has small hairs tangled up in it that are now falling onto my lap.

"What the hell, that is super creepy and gross," I say as I show the camera our first find.

The second thing I reach in for is a little wooden jar, handmade, with a weird symbol carved into the top. I show Brooklyn and the handheld camera my findings.

"It looks like the wood is carved with a symbol of a regular triangle. Below that is an upside-down triangle almost touching with a huge 'x' going through both of them."

I start to open the small wooden box, and it catches on the lip. I pull harder. Teeth in every shape and size clatter to the floor and onto the table.

"Be careful!" Brooklyn says, looking like she's about to go ghost white.

"It's okay," I say as I reach back in the box, leaving the teeth to find after the video.

"Your turn, Brooklyn," I say as I take the small handheld camera out of her hand and start filming.

She pulls out a picture of a house in the middle of some train tracks. In the picture is what looks like a family sitting on a porch. One older man with salt and pepper hair, a girl with curly brown hair and jeans on, an older boy with slicked-back black hair, and another boy, bald, that looks like he's looking straight passed the camera.

"Oh my god, that's Parker in the picture! That delivery person!" I say and point to the person in the picture.

"The picture is so blurry, I can't tell if that's just a bald kid or actually Parker from YouTube, but it's such a stretch, it could just be a random person." Brooklyn says.

On the back of the picture, it looks like there's latitude and longitude coordinates.

"Let's Google this real fast." I say and pull out my phone.

"It looks like a random place in the middle of Denver, Colorado. Weird."

Brooklyn shrugs and pulls out a damp cloth; blood is seeping through the fabric. This is where the smell is coming from. She unwraps it, and inside is a sawed-off ear. She throws it down onto the table and screams.

"Okay, it's probably fake. Let's look closer. No need to freak out yet. We knew this might happen," I say calmly.

The cartilage was pierced with wire and a note that says 'HP'. Brooklyn reaches in the box, and there's another piece of bloodied cloth, this one wrapped around a sawed-off toe. The toe had a tag on it like a present under the Christmas tree. The tag had two initials: "JH"

"Okay, this is fucked up, Kai. Who the hell is sending us body parts like this?!"

"There're only two more things left in here. Let's just get through it."

All of our commentary is out the window. One because we literally can't breathe with the rotting smell of the body parts, even with the masks, and two, I'm starting to get a bad feeling Parker and Hayden received the same box and something happened to them.

I reach in and pull out a GoPro camera, but the lens is shattered and it won't turn on. It looks like it could just strap around a body like Ghost Hunters do when they're in an abandoned building. I don't think much of it until the last item in the box is a small thumb drive.

"Let's get the computer out and put it in. We have to see what's on it."

Honestly, I'm a little disappointed with how few things there are in the box, fake or not. Brooklyn grabs the computer and inserts the thumb drive. It's of course password protected.

"What the fuck are we supposed to do with this? We literally were given no clues or numbers besides the coordinates." Brooklyn says in a frustrated tone.

"I have no clue." I say as I lean back on the couch and put my hands over my eyes.

I stare at the ceiling, thinking to myself that it wants a four-number combination. The coordinates are multiple numbers, and there's no way they pertain to it. I can hear Brooklyn start typing in random number combinations thinking she may get lucky, but I know that's not going to happen. Not with our luck. Then I think back through the entire day. I've always had a great memory. Maybe it's always been the trauma in my brain, but instead of protecting me to forget it, I'm destined to remember it my entire life. Whoever was delivering the package asked if this address was 1358 Morrison Lane, but those numbers aren't even close to the real address. They would've been all the way across town, as the street goes on for miles. I sit up, go to the computer and type in the simple numbers 1358 and the file opens.

"How the hell?" Brooklyn starts to ask.

"I'll explain later," I say as I press play on the video.

The video was shot from someone's chest and edited. The sounds were cut together in awkward English. You couldn't understand anything they were saying. The picture flickers to a parking lot and shows Jameson and Hayden from the Put Up or Shut Up YouTube channel and a girl that I've never seen before. They get into a Blue Jeep and head down the road until it cuts to the house in the picture from the mystery box. The sound of the video keeps distorting to high pitched laughter to deep voices talking, but still, you couldn't understand a thing they're saying. They reach the house and find that the porch is carved with the same symbol we just saw on the wooden homemade box.

They split up. It looks like they're fighting.

It suddenly cuts to Jameson's throat being slit and bleeding out onto the floor. The static is taking up most of the tape. It then cuts to a scene where you can see Hayden tied up on some pews, she looks sick. The static forms and it cuts back to everyone giving each other high fives in the parking lot before getting into the Jeep. Suddenly you can see from the camera angle on the chest a giant statue of the symbol and a man with salt and pepper hair staring at what looks like a double-helix biblical angel. He's talking to it in a tongue we don't understand. The creature was indescribable. Almost looked like black feathers and skin going in and out of itself. The picture on the screen was fading in and out and, with so much static, you could barely see anything else but a glimpse of its many eyes. The video cuts to Hayden smiling on top of a beautiful mountain laughing. Static builds and you can see a Hayden back in the pews tied up and then a tattooed hand put a knife in her heart and twist. Hayden's eyes go wide; she falls as the knife is pulled back out. The video ends with a whole minute of a blooded tattooed hand dripping the hot red liquid down their arm onto the floor. I almost turn off the video there until it looks like a black screen where in a normal movie the credits would start rolling. All it says in white letters is.

Want to know more?

Come find me :)

Acknowledgments

First off, I want to thank my amazing partner, Emily, for listening to my idea about this novel and telling me to just start writing it. You will never understand how much your support encourages me to chase these silly dreams of mine.

Thank you, Jorie, for coming along with me on this journey, working countless hours, and for being one of my best friends since elementary school. You have helped me more than you know and I hope this is a beautiful start to a long partnership in creating books that appease our taste in horror.

Thank you to all of my grandparents for reading chapter after chapter of the sloppy first draft and giving me your honest input. It kept me focused and helped me push this book forward to completion.

Thank you to the talented Jess Smith and Nick Bonney for helping me get the artwork and stickers perfect for the release. Jess, you have no idea how awesome and easy you are to work with. It seems like you went into my brain and saw exactly what I wanted and just used your magic to make it come to fruition.

Thank you to my mother for reading half of the book ;) and giving me solid advice over and over again. I hope this book makes you proud as an avid horror fan.

Thank you, Jacob, for being my printing master and helping me cut out the rough parts to the blurb on the back. It became perfect with your help and attention.

Thank you to my pup Obi for being patient (as best he could) while I spent countless hours on my laptop when he wanted to play.

Last, but not least, I'm truly thankful for you, the reader, for spending your hard-earned money to buy a book from a small queer artist with no effing clue what they're doing. You are the ones that are making my dreams a reality. I literally cannot do this without your ongoing support.

Hope you all enjoyed reading *The Mystery Box*!

Made in the USA
Middletown, DE
21 June 2024

55846222R00109